More books by Donna Huston Murray

The Ginger Barnes Main Line Mysteries:

THE MAIN LINE IS MURDER + audio
FINAL ARRANGEMENTS + audio
SCHOOL OF HARD KNOCKS
NO BONES ABOUT IT
A SCORE TO SETTLE
FAREWELL PERFORMANCE (e-book pending)
LIE LIKE A RUG
FOR BETTER OR WORSE
Finalist, National Indie Excellence Award, Mysteries

The Lauren Beck Crime Novels:

WHAT DOESN'T KILL YOU
Writer's Digest Honorable Mention in genre fiction 2015
GUILT TRIP
Writer's Digest Honorable Mention in genre fiction 2018
DOUBLE DOWN
The Lauren Beck Crime Novels #1 and #2 Bundle
STRANGER DANGER

A Traditional Mystery:

DYING FOR A VACATION

STRANGER DANGER

A LAUREN BECK CRIME NOVEL

DONNA HUSTON MURRAY

Ravenhill
Press

STRANGER DANGER
Copyright 2023 by Donna Huston Murray
ISBN #978-1-7365446-1-7
All rights reserved.

This is a work of fiction. Names, characters, places, and incidents are either the product of the author's imagination or are used fictitiously. Any similarity to real persons, living or dead, is coincidental and not intended by the author.

All rights reserved. No part of this book may be used or reproduced in any manner whatsoever without express written permission of the author except in the case of brief quotations embodied in critical articles or reviews.

You are invited to contact the author at:
donnahustonmurray.com

Cover by Michelle Argyle with
Melissa Williams Design

DEDICATION

This book can only be dedicated to **Joe Geiser**, a high school classmate of mine who, much to my astonishment, nominated me for our school's highest honor. Thanks to him and the two committees he coaxed onboard, I am now the tenth inductee into **North Penn's Lifetime Achievement Hall of Fame**. No words can sufficiently express my gratitude.

—Donna

Chapter 1

SO I'M CRUISING along, top down, sunscreen on, Ray-Bans, my blonde ponytail flicking back and forth like some carefree model in a feminine hygiene commercial, and oh no! Losing power, Major Tom. Losing *all* power.

I climb out, lift the Miata's hood, and recoil from a steaming, stinky cloud of smoke.

"Why?" I ask the ancient engine. "Why now?" We are perhaps forty miles from my destination. Maybe not even.

Sadly, the answer is all too obvious. I've been driving hard ever since I left Maryland. We are surrounded by cacti baking in the sand. If there was a whiff of a breeze, I'm sure tumbleweed would be rolling by. My sweet ride chose the perfect place to make her point.

Fifty ways to leave your lover, one of them a tow truck.

I dig out my cell phone and hope for a signal.

Yes! We aren't as far from civilization as I feared. Now that I think about it, not that far back was a cluster of businesses, a hint of habitation. Electricity. Running water. Humans...

AAA asks if I'm safe. "For a short time," I reply truthfully. "It's pretty hot, and there isn't any shelter." Putting the black ragtop up and waiting inside the car would be stifling, worse than staying out in the open air.

"Copy that," remarks the dispatcher. "On it right away."

I grab a bottle of lukewarm water from the console and dig an Orioles cap out of the trunk. Pocket my phone. Look around. There isn't much to see, just a billboard forty yards away. It's casting a feeble late afternoon shadow in my direction, so I fan myself with the hat and stroll toward it. The tow truck driver will have no problem finding me.

That the sign is there at all strikes me as odd. The wooden frame looks old but is well preserved by the New Mexico climate. Still, I can't imagine who would bother advertising in such a lonely spot. A struggling enterprise, for sure. Someone in need of a bargain.

When I get to the shade, I kick a lump of stone away with my sneaker and draw a swipe in the sand with my toe. I planned to live off my savings short term, and now I'm worried what the Miata's going to cost.

No point in moping about that now. I lift my head to give the billboard a closer look and immediately feel worse.

The photo is of a young girl in jeans and a pink t-shirt, sitting on a blanket. Her left leg is outstretched, her right pulled up. Her torso is twisted toward the camera, and her reluctant smile tells me she's indulging whichever parent holds the camera. The desert sun has bleached the sign enough to make her features appear indistinct and her complexion paler than it should. Yet her hair is clearly auburn, her eyes most likely hazel or blue. Her approximate age thirteen.

Kathleen Duncan. I memorize her name out of respect, as if keeping it in my head will somehow prolong her existence. For she is missing. The phone number printed in a huge, black font begs for information leading to her whereabouts. To an ex-cop like me, the billboard says "abduction" and suggests this beautiful young girl is dead.

It's times like this, when I'm distressed by something else, that my most haunting failure rears up. Standing in the literal shadow of another missing child, I suppose I should have seen it coming.

It wasn't as if my head hadn't been in the game. Or I was drunk and not paying attention. Or my partner was a dope. Or any of the excuses you see on TV. I just didn't find her in time. I got to the shed behind the church first, which was why I saw the pile of boards covering her tender, bruised body before anyone else. Lifting the last jagged piece of plywood gave me enough nightmare material to last a lifetime.

Patty Lennon, resting in peace no thanks to me.

Knowing the child on the billboard probably suffered a similar fate has sharpened my senses with desperate life. I feel the sweat on my neck, taste the stale, warm water from the car, sweep away the tickle of hair from across my cheek. As always, I ache for the victim's family and wish there was something I could do for them.

Survivor's guilt? Probably just plain guilt.

A few cars have driven past at speeds ranging from in-no-hurry to my-foot's-on-fire. None showed one speck of interest in my predicament, so I'm especially relieved when a truck spelling out "Tommy's Towing" in gold-shadowed script lumbers to a stop in front of the Miata.

"Hi. I'm Lauren Beck," I say, extending my hand. "Thanks for coming."

A large, stoop-shouldered man emerges from the cab and lifts a quizzical eyebrow.

"You must be Tommy," I add, which is when I notice the "Ned" label on his shirt.

Ned lets that revelation settle in before he enters the conversation.

"Just quit on ya, eh?"

"Yep. She, uh, pretty much just stopped running."

Resting his grease-blackened hands on the warm edge of the Miata's engine well, my rescuer spits a stream of chewing tobacco into the dust at the side of the road.

Shaking his head, he drops the hood shut, repositions the tobacco, and fixes me with a woeful stare.

"You in a hurry?" he asks.

I shrug.

When we last spoke, my father perked up at the idea of a visit. But he didn't offer a date, and I couldn't bring myself to admit I was homeless again. I dithered about calling to say I'm on my way, but the closer I got to New Mexico the more a good, old-fashioned surprise appealed to me. I pictured Dad's smile stretching to his ears, me stepping into his warm hug...

Ned seems to sense ambivalence.

"Best thing'd be take 'er to CarMaster," he decides for me. "They can fix most anything, and if they can't, they got used vehicles plenty newer than this out the whazoo. Sound good to you?"

"No. I mean yes. They nearby?"

Ned ejects the last of the tobacco into the dust. "What d'you care?" His lip lifts at the corner, and I huff out a laugh.

"They got a Coke machine?"

"Yup. A clean ladies' room, too."

He goes about the business of cranking my darling red convertible onto the back of the truck, and soon we're side by side going back the way I came.

Ned defaults into a tight-lipped silence, as if driving a loaded tow truck is absorbing enough for him. No soul-wrenching Western radio music. Not even a lame joke about the weather.

Miles go by at a snail's pace with nothing to keep me from obsessing about the reception I'll get from my father and his new wife. Ana sounds quite nice. But stepmothers, especially ones with a kid of their own, don't always cotton to their new spouse's progeny.

I really should have warned Dad I was coming.

"Mind if I use my phone?" I inquire.

Ned shoots me an up-to-you glance and returns his eyes to the road.

I open my Contacts and poke Dad's home number.

After fifteen rings, I end the call.

Great, I think to myself. *Something else to worry about.*

Chapter 2

THE USED-CAR SALESMAN wears a summer weight, baby-blue sport coat and gestures with a manicured hand. "I'm gonna be honest, hon. Your Miata's toast." To emphasize his sincerity, he lowers his chin and meets my stare.

Seeing my savings go up in smoke, I stifle a four-letter word.

"Okay. Show me what you got," I reluctantly tell the salesman I mentally call Ernie, for aren't all overachieving used-car salesmen Ernest no matter what their mother named them?

His lips curl, and his eyes gleam. "What's your price range?" he asks, as he shrugs out of the sport coat. The air conditioning inside is frigid, the outside temperature another story altogether.

I let him interpret my shrug however he wants.

His eyelids lower. "C'mon, hon. Ballpark figure."

I shrug again, and his lips press tight.

We saunter outside. Strolling through the heat is like wading through pudding.

"How about this beauty, hon," Ernie urges. "Only ninety-five thousand on it and rarin' to go."

It is the size of a parade float and emits stale cigarette stink the instant the door is opened.

"Nope," I reply, and begin to hustle down the row.

Ernie trots to keep up. "Can you at least tell me what you're looking for?"

"Know it when I see it."

Two rows later, I stop at an orange Jeep. It has a rag roof across the back and comfy-looking dark gray seats. I know Jeeps to be a bit expensive, but good quality. However, I assume this one is here for a reason.

"Uh," Ernie waffles. "That's not for sale."

Which is when I notice we strayed into the employee parking lot.

I figure a dealership employee probably takes good care of his ride. It is also the only Jeep in sight, suggesting its owner prefers anything but the company's everyday stock.

My lips lift into a mischievous smile. "Would the owner consider an offer?"

"I…I…"

"Why don't you ask?"

"Ummm…"

While "Ernie" plods back to the showroom, I take the opportunity to engage my brain. My usual outdoor activities are running and hiking. This model offers enough room for what little I brought with me, and if I ever need to sleep in my car again, *God forbid,* I can manage just fine.

Short story. It belongs to the boss, a florid, paunchy male specimen who obviously doesn't run or hike or camp or anything remotely sporty, so he probably has no business driving a Jeep. Also, according to Ernie's sly whisper, boss-man switches cars as often as twice a year.

On the requisite test drive, I discover I like the Jeep's solid feel. Probably the same reason it bucked like a bronc when I drove over a speed bump. I mentally name my new ride Buck, borrow a computer to transfer my precious savings to my checking account, read the fine print, sign up, pay up, and resign myself to pouring dirty martinis to pinstriped customers for the foreseeable future.

This, plus the ritual used-car clean-out and clean-up, takes us up to dinnertime. At last, Buck has finally come to a halt in the exit tunnel next to the glass door adjacent to the sales floor.

Bouncing the keys on his greasy glove, the man who just prettied up my purchase hops out and enters the showroom. When he lifts his chin to look at me, his shoulders jerk as if I've stopped him with both hands. His mouth gapes and a vivid blush ignites his southwestern sun-dweller's tan. I note that his earlobes have an unusual squared-off shape as if they've been trimmed. Ridiculous, of course, but something I've seen at least once before. His eyes might be chocolate brown, but he lifted his face so briefly I can't say for sure.

I'm young and athletic, I'm blonde, and I have breasts. Currently they are encased in a red and white striped tank top because I've been alone in my now defunct red convertible driving diagonally across the country. Tons of people along the way will never see me again, so I haven't worried about overdoing the blonde thing.

However, I was a cop. I should know better than to invite unwanted attention.

The car mechanic's head angles sideways and down as if to deny his reaction. His gloved fist closes around the Jeep's keys. He mumbles, "Forgot something. Be right back."

Pivoting on his bootheels, he pushes the glass door wide enough to waltz through without crashing into the doorjamb. After hoisting his ass up onto the Jeep's driver's seat, he roars out of the drop-off tunnel straight down the short driveway and out onto the road.

"Did he just steal my car?" I ask, only half joking.

"He'll be right back," Ernie says, his face as gray as oatmeal.

Chapter 3

LOUELLA SPIT THE FIRST mouthful of Bammy's oatmeal back into the bowl. The oatmeal she'd had at her friend Charlotte's house tasted like cookies. This stuff was so salty she wanted to barf.

"Aaaaah," her grandmother cried out, warning the six-year-old she should have swallowed like she did when Bammy gave her chicken with stuff on it that burned her tongue.

Gray hair flying free from its pins, spoon raised toward the ceiling, her grandmother was huffing back and forth.

Louella pushed away from the table in case she needed to run. God was about to get another "What'd I do to deserve this?" scolding from Bammy. That was for sure.

Then suddenly the old woman's pacing stopped. The spoon landed back in the pot, and Bammy whirled to face her late daughter's daughter. Fists resting on ample hips, she aimed an ugly glare at Louella's widened eyes.

"I'm sick and tired of your ingratitude, young lady. No party for little girls that don't eat their oatmeal. Time you learnt some respect."

"But I'm all ready to go," Louella pleaded.

"I said no, Missy."

"It's not fair."

Bammy reached for the wooden spoon, and Louella jumped off the chair.

"Go'on now. Scat."

"I didn't have any breakfast."

"Yes, you did. You jus' din't eat it."

Tears stung in Louella's eyes, which would not do. She was too old to cry like a baby over missing breakfast. She ran upstairs and dug two cookies she'd brought home from Sunday school out of their hiding spot. Whenever possible, she tried to have her own food. Living with Bammy had taught her that. She also knew to brush the crumbs off her bedspread.

"Not fair," she whispered to herself as the tears began to drip. "Super not fair."

And then it came to her. She would wait for Bammy to come up to use the bathroom, then sneak downstairs and out the door. Charlotte's mother wouldn't mind if she was early. Mrs. Ramsey might even let her phone her father. He drove a truck cross-country, so he wasn't home. But if she asked real nice, maybe she could stay at Charlotte's until her dad got back. Then he would grin at her so hard he'd get deep wrinkles on each side of his mouth. He would laugh, and hug her, and pet her hair, and tell her she never had to eat salty oatmeal ever again.

When she heard the heavy march of her grandmother coming upstairs, Louella sniffled extra loud on purpose until the bathroom door shut tight.

Then she slipped down the stairs quiet as a cat and out the front door.

It was nice out, with few clouds and no need for a jacket. Lucky, because she didn't bring a thing with her. Not even Charlotte's present, a dusty old Perfection game Bammy found at the church basement sale.

The pavement was cracked and bumpy, so Louella tried hard not to scuff her almost-new, basement-sale shoes. Around her, birds talked bird business in the trees, and through one window of the close-set houses a TV flickered with morning cartoons. A teenage boy played noisy music on his phone while he washed a car, but otherwise nobody seemed to be around.

Louella was careful crossing the street in between blocks, but pretty soon the blocks began to look strange. She hugged her elbows with her hands and hurried. Charlotte's house had to be right up ahead, maybe farther than she thought, but it was there.

Wasn't it?

Her lower lip began to tremble, and her steps slowed.

That was when the blue car stopped beside her, and the closest window rolled down.

The man driving leaned away from the steering wheel to speak to her.

"Hello, little girl. That's a pretty dress you've got on, but you shouldn't be out here by yourself. Are you lost?"

Chapter 4

I'VE JUST PURCHASED a bottle of water from the dealership's vending machine when the mechanic returns with my Jeep.

Loaded for bear and waiting by the exit-tunnel's glass door, the boss corrals his errant employee as soon as he enters. Ernie the Salesman hovers close by, an eager audience.

I'm too far away to hear, but the boss is obviously delivering a finger-wagging lecture. Arms spread, a telltale white bag dangling from his hand, the mechanic tries to defend himself.

A few steps back, Ernie has fidgeted around enough to see me wave. After a last glance at the show, he steams toward me with hands on his waist and blue jacket flapping.

"Something else," he mutters. "Never seen nothin' like it."

"What's the story?"

The salesman shakes his head. "He panicked. Was supposed to pick up his girlfriend's prescription yesterday. Something he says she needs every day."

"Birth control?" I wonder aloud, and Ernie snickers.

"Guess that'd do it."

"You think he'll get fired?"

"Nah. Too good a mechanic. Rollie's just givin' him hell for screwing up."

"Keys?" I remind him.

"In the ignition."

On my way past, I wave the paperwork envelope at the men in lieu of goodbye. This late in the day, getting to Dad and Ana's house at a civilized hour may be impossible. Not the sort of surprise I had in mind.

Forty minutes later, I arrive at their suburban cottage in the fresh glow of twilight.

The one-story house is pale stucco with a Spanish tile roof, the distance to a strikingly blue front door fifteen feet at most. A curb would allow one car to park, but the spot is just packed clay at the moment.

Nobody answers my knock on the door; and, since only an NBA player could to see through the small, decorative rectangle of glass at the top, I sidle across the arid earth to the right front window, shield my eyes, and peek in.

Lots of shadows. No lights.

The solid, six-foot-high wooden fence encasing the back yard is the same earthy, flower-pot brown as the roof. Its gate is padlocked, making me wonder whether the neighborhood is the safe little enclave it appears to be.

I call my father's cell.

Fifteen rings. No answer.

My heart is beating hard now. My hands are slick with sweat. I'm imagining my dad as sick, injured…or worse.

And what about Ana? Could she be sick or injured, too?

I give myself a hard mental shake. It's past dinnertime; I am hungry myself. Maybe Dad and his young bride went out to eat. But no lights? This street will be dark as a cavern pretty soon.

Lights have come on straight across the street. None yet in the nearby homes.

Across the street it is.

A dog barks even before my knuckles tap the door.

The middle-aged woman who answers is wiping her hands on a dishtowel. She's got wispy tan hair secured behind her head and eyes that could melt metal. Her peephole is eye-level, and I feel certain she used it.

"Yes?" she asks. "Is there a problem?"

Good guess, considering the hour.

"I'm Bernie Beck's daughter, Lauren. Have you seen my dad or his wife today?"

The neighbor thinks for a moment.

"Now that you mention it, Raffles did hear their car leave."

The yappy dog. Of course. *Good dog.*

"About when was that?"

"Yesterday?"

Not good.

"By any chance do you have a key to the house? I'd like to make sure everything's okay."

"Wouldn't let you in even if I did. Never saw you before in my life, have I?"

Unfortunately, she has a point.

Okay. So if she and the Beck couple across-the-street aren't friendly enough to exchange emergency keys, maybe someone else has one. Or else Dad hid a spare.

More homes have lights on now, and an additional car sits along the curb just past the Jeep. Darkness is nearly complete, so I poke on my phone's flashlight to hunt around Dad and Ana's doorway for a spare key.

I've just bent down to look under the mat when a man tackles me sideways. My phone illuminates fat, spatulate fingers reaching for my throat while the attacker's stocky body nearly crushes me flat on the cement landing. The impact sends my phone flying.

Struggling to reach the thug's crotch, my hand encounters what feels like a long canvas jacket—over sweatpants, according to my bare leg.

Adrenaline pumping, I roll onto my side, free an arm, and slam my palm hard up under his chin.

The thug rears back.

I push myself into a sit. He rams my shoulder into the front door. My head snaps hard enough to put stars in the sky.

I glimpse a windup that would put me out for sure, except suddenly floodlights bright enough to light a prison yard have started blinking like crazy and an alarm is screaming loud enough to wake the dead.

My attacker heaves himself up and runs to the car at the curb. Three seconds later it takes off as if somebody already had a foot on the gas.

I stagger around to the front of the Jeep but only glimpse a yellow license plate with maybe red letters and the hint of a Honda emblem glinting off dark paint. An Accord, probably. As common as cactus.

With the usual fanfare, the cops arrive just as I find my phone.

Chapter 5

THE SECURITY COMPANY shut off the light/alarm circus remotely. The police who responded look at what there is to see—the lump on my head, the minor scrapes on my arms and knees. They write notes, ask if I want to file a formal report.

Hell, yes, I do.

"Then please follow us to the station. It isn't far."

Soon I am sitting in front of an officer's desk elucidating my concerns. Namely, that my father and Ana aren't home and probably haven't been for a day. So where are they? Also, why the fancy security? And—elephant in the room—why was I attacked on their doorstep? My purse wasn't stolen, and I wasn't really harmed. Failed abduction attempt? A potential rape?

"I just don't get it." I summarize for the gentleman in uniform with his elbows on a littered desk centered in a small office. He is a fit man of perhaps fifty. Clean shaven. Neat hands. Reading glasses at the ready. Stained white coffee mug within reach. His name is Robert Dobbs, but he invited me to call him Sarge purely from habit. I know, because it's the same ruse I used to simulate friendship. His actual attitude seems to be impatience laced with irritation.

"Here's the thing, Lauren, if I may call you that. The alarm wasn't the only notice we got about you tonight."

"Oh?"

"Yes. Neighbor across the street mentioned your interest in getting inside an empty house."

"So, what did she do? Hire a thug to get rid of me?"

Sarge huffs out a dry laugh. "You got any proof you're the homeowner's daughter?"

"My name?"

"I suppose there is that. Except how come you didn't know your dad is away?"

"I wanted to surprise him."

"All the way from the east coast? Helluva chancy surprise, wouldn't you say?"

Don't rub it in...

"How's this?" he adds, as he actually twiddles his thumbs. "I think you'll agree, you don't see many orange cars. So, tell me this. Why're you driving Rollie Holcroft's orange Jeep? Rollie's a personal friend, and I know for a fact he had that vehicle in his possession last Sunday."

So now I'm a car thief and a burglar?

"I bought it from Rollie this afternoon."

"Put up much of a fight, did he?"

"Not too much. Where are you going with this?"

"Just curious who you are and why you wanted to get inside that house so bad. What with your father being out of town and all."

"Oh, for goodness sake. He's my father. I wanted to be sure he was okay."

"And his wife, too, of course."

"Of course. Although, for all I know, one of them just took the car out, and the other was..."

"What?"

"Hurt or something."

"Why would you think that?"

"Maybe because I was a cop, and cops tend to think that way?"

"You don't look like a cop."

Again, I realize I am wearing a red and white striped tank top, shorts, and probably goose bumps. If the New

Mexico locals like being cold so much, why don't they live in Alaska?

"Where were you a cop?"

"Landis, Pennsylvania."

"Can you prove it?"

"If you insist." Scarp Poletta is my remaining friend on the force, a homicide detective built like a Clydesdale with whom I had a brief "thing." Sadly, my neuroses were not interesting enough to hold him. He returned to a basket-case named Rainy McQuinn.

Scarp does not welcome my phone calls.

Hoping to steer the conversation in a more productive direction, I remind "Sarge" I was mugged. "You planning on doing anything about that?"

He pretends to think it over.

"Any weapon involved?"

"Just brute force."

"Hmmm. Anything stolen?"

I shake my head. "When I got knocked into the door, Dad's alarm was loud enough to scare off Godzilla."

"So, that's a no. You hurt?"

"Not much," I admit.

We stare at each other for a long second. Me with narrowed eyes and my lips pressed tight. Him with a smug grin I'd like to punch.

"You planning on doing anything…about anything?" I ask.

Dobbs leans back and clears his throat.

"Well, let's see. You were…what shall we say?…knocked down by a man you can't describe who really didn't hurt you or take anything. Your dad and his wife haven't been reported as missing. You aren't reporting them missing, are you?"

I hold my tongue.

"Didn't think so. So, what exactly would you like me to do?"

It is past time for me to leave.

Rising, I notice an orange cupcake hidden behind a pile of paperwork. Since orange confections this long before Halloween are uncommon, I view it as a sign. I'm hungry, and this jerk has wasted at least a cupcake's worth of my time.

"Can I have that?"

Dobbs follows my gaze and catches on immediately.

"No," he replies with some pleasure, I suppose because he feels I wasted his time, too. Or else he's also hungry, which might account for his mood.

I heft my saddlebag purse onto my shoulder, turn for the door, and draw up short.

Standing there is a tree-trunk of a man with a note in his hand. His features have been chiseled by a chain saw, and I've never seen a better fit on a uniform. I immediately want to flee.

Sarge begins to introduce us. Backwards if you subscribe to the ladies-first rule.

"Chief, this is Ms. Beck. Ms. Beck, Chief Jenkins."

The tree trunk extends his right hand, so I allow him to grab hold of mine. Unfortunately, that slides my loaded purse off my left shoulder, and I have to withdraw from the grasp to adjust the strap of my tank top.

Chief chuckles.

I may be blushing, but I hope not. Normally, I'm not that modest.

"Jack," the living, breathing cigar-store Indian, announces his first name.

"I've gotta go," I hint.

"Stay a minute," Sarge encourages from behind his desk. "Maybe the chief will have another take on your predicament."

When I turn to shoot him a glare, Dobbs is licking a blob of orange icing off his fingertips, and I feel my eyebrows clench.

"Oh?" Jack queries. He's smiling, but he's also blocking my escape.

Donning a smug attitude I suspect he uses often, Sarge sets the cupcake aside in order to summarize. First, the mugging. Then the call about a suspicious woman trying to get inside a house with nobody home.

"It belongs to my father," I remark in self-defense. "Also, I'm former police. I assume the worst by default."

Jack's expression softens to something resembling sympathy. "Why don't we give Sarge here a chance to take care of the problem I just handed him? We can talk in my office."

I balk. Now that I know nothing is going to be done, I want out of there. "I missed dinner," I say by way of an excuse.

"This'll only take a minute. I'm interested in why you were attacked."

Me, too. Come to think of it.

The chief's office is clean and modern. Cluttered enough to suggest work is getting done. Just big enough for half a dozen officers to gather for instructions, if they remain standing.

"Make yourself comfortable." He indicates a visitor's chair with the sweep of his hand.

"You have any mittens I can borrow?"

Jack gives that a tolerant grin, which immediately defaults to quizzical.

"Tell me details."

I accept the offered chair, then quickly itemize my day, including the car mechanic bugging out with my newly purchased Jeep, ostensibly on an emergency trip to the drug store.

Jack waves his head as if marveling at the peculiar things people do and the dumb reasons they do them.

As I finish my report, I notice a family photo over Chief Jenkins's shoulder and feel myself relax.

Don't get me wrong. Most men, no problem. But ever since my uber-photogenic fiancé dumped me—the day after I was diagnosed with Hodgkin's Disease—I've had an aversion to pretty men. Knowing some other woman joined Jack Jenkins at the altar years ago? Perfect. No temptation either way.

It feels good, telling him why I'm so worried about my father. After all, I did nothing to invite a thug to attack me except knock on Dad's door.

I hear myself pouring out details, like how close my father and I were while I was growing up without a mother. But then he moved to New Mexico, and we grew apart.

"That's why I'm here," I admit to this complete stranger. "To close the gap."

A final sort of silence falls, which is when the man I just met asks, "So where're you staying tonight?"

Chapter 6

I'M THINKING, "Excuse me?" which probably shows.

"Allow me to start over," Jack Jenkins hastily amends. "You expected to stay at your dad's, didn't you." A statement, not a question.

"That isn't why I was trying to get inside, you know. I have a credit card."

"But…?"

"…but I bought a car today."

"Ah, yes. Kick in the savings, isn't it?"

"No worries. I can bartend anywhere anytime."

"In your case, I see that's true, but that won't help you tonight." He thinks a moment. "How about staying here?"

"Whutdaya mean, stay here? In a cell?"

The Chief of Police chuckles. Points to a sofa I hadn't noticed.

"Oh." I swivel back to look him in the eye. "You want to keep an eye on me, right." Also, not a question.

"Well…"

"The friend on the Landis police force who can vouch for me is named Scarp Poletta." I recite Scarp's cell phone number.

"Nobody else?"

"It's been a while. People forget."

"Why'd you leave?"

"None of your business."

"Hodgkin's disease?"

My jaw drops. There hasn't been time for him to look into me yet. "How'd you…?"

All traces of this-is-fun banter are gone. "When you…" He pinches his uniform in front of his armpit and wiggles the fabric.

The scars. When I lifted my tank top strap back in place, he noticed the scars from my surgery.

"My sister," he explains before I ask.

"She okay?"

"Yeah, thanks. Yes, she's fine."

"Any kids?" Not my place to ask, but it is my Achilles heel, the remaining after-effect that most affects my future—and my present behavior. Because of a glitch in my treatment, no children for me.

"She had two before."

I nod to disguise the lump in my throat.

Jack Jenkins looks away, perhaps recalling his sister's ordeal. Applying it to me.

"That's rough," he remarks. "Glad to see you've recovered."

"Thanks."

When the moment becomes uncomfortable, I blurt, "I'm starving. I should have grabbed that cupcake when I had the chance."

Jack throws up his hands. "Oh, lord. I'm sorry. Shall I order a pizza?"

"Shouldn't you be going home?" I lift my chin to indicate the wife and kids in the photo over his shoulder.

"After the pizza. Least I can do."

"Yeah, but shouldn't you be going home?"

He pauses as if I've trespassed too far into personal territory, but answers anyway. "I like to stick around some nights. Keep an eye on things."

"Gotcha." He's a good boss, a good, responsible boss.

Our eyes meet. Not in a romantic way, I assure you. The better way. Between two human beings who appreciate that they're both human beings.

We agree on half mushroom, half plain, and he phones it in.

"Borrow the keys to your Jeep?" he asks casually. "We should move it if you'll be here overnight."

I start to stand. "Where do you want it?"

"No, no. Sit. Pizza'll be here any minute. Let Sarge get it."

I stand anyway. "If you don't mind, I'd like to get some stuff out first."

"Oh, sure. Didn't think of that."

So, what happens is I go and dig out clothes and personal things for overnight and tomorrow morning, check on the Glock, return to the lobby, which is already secured for the night, hand Sarge my keys, and arrive back in time for hot pizza and vending machine soda.

We eat in silence, until I think to ask about the billboard girl, Kathleen Duncan, who's been on my mind off and on all day. "Please tell me you found her."

"Still open," my host admits, the pain of regret creasing his forehead.

Far more fragile than when I was back on the job, I'm flooded with emotion I once knew how to suppress. Still, I do my best to behave like my former self. I ask what all they've done to find Kathleen. I ask how the parents are holding up, and I listen intently to Jack's answers.

"I gather you've had a case like that yourself," he concludes.

I nod.

"And…?"

I wave my head no.

Jack says nothing. Just turns and stares into the far, far distance. I am already there myself, in the shed behind the church lifting a last piece of plywood.

My appetite is pretty shot now, but since it's here, I snag the last slice of mushroom. Stuffing myself seems preferable to anymore shop talk.

Jack folds the empty box and shoves it into his wastebasket. Then he takes me to see the women's locker room. Though small, it contains all the usual fixtures, including a shower.

"I'll leave it unlocked," he informs me, which summons an uncomfortable thought.

As trusted as I seemingly am, the premises will be populated by the usual overnight staff. In other words, I won't exactly be unobserved.

Then there is the matter of my car, which Sarge locked up tight in the station's evidence lot.

I am no more free to leave than if I were in a cell.

That certainty is underscored by our return to the Chief's office. Standing with his feet apart and his hands behind his back, Sarge acknowledges his boss with a curt nod. Then he directs the entirety of his considerable sternness toward me.

In hindsight, I'm sure he choreographed his performance, because it was impeccable.

His right hand swung forward dramatically and tossed me the keys to the Jeep.

Then, for maximum effect, his left hand came around slowly to reveal the Glock I had in my duffel.

"You got a license for this?" he asks with nasty glee.

Curtain and applause.

Chapter 7

BEFORE JACK LEAVES, he scrounges up a scratchy gray blanket and a pillow with a cover so new it feels starched. I try not to let the probability that they came from a cell bother me, or the fact that his office sofa is a bit short for my five-foot-eight. I am inordinately grateful for the free accommodation, the shower, the pizza, and for generally being treated with any consideration at all. The searching of my car and locking me in I mostly blame on Dobbs. You do need suspicious jerks like him on the force. After all, they're often right.

I am awakened in the morning by Jack's arrival. Sun floods the room from an uncovered window, and dust motes seem to swirl with joy.

The Chief of Police hands me a McDonald's bag smelling of McMuffin and coffee. "Here, breakfast," he says, as if reluctantly fulfilling an obligation.

I've been sleeping in sweatpants to fend off both the air conditioning and the bimbo impression of yesterday's outfit. To accept the bag, I push the scratchy blanket aside and swing my feet to the floor.

"What's going on?" I ask carefully. Maybe his grandmother is sick, or somebody he liked got killed.

Maybe they found Kathleen Duncan's body.

None of the above.

"Scarp Poletta vouched for you," Jack remarks, as if it's of very little importance. As if *I* am of very little importance, which from his viewpoint is surely true. "FYI, don't call to thank him. He's on his honeymoon."

Jack is watching my face, so I say, "Okay. Okay, good," but I'm wrestling with a stab of disappointment over the news, striving for a smidgen of happiness for Scarp and Rainy. Relief that my honesty is no longer in question hasn't yet made it to the table.

I cover by putting on my sneakers.

Walking around to his black, ergonomic chair, Jack taps his desk with his knuckles. Settling back, he tents his fingers just below a thoughtful pout.

"What's going on?" I repeat.

"There's a car in your father's driveway."

"Good. Thanks. That's great. What else?"

"So, you can go now. Okay?"

"Sure, sure…" He is the Chief of Police. He has work to do—always—and he wants to get on with it.

But…

"Wait a minute," I blurt. "You didn't tell my dad…?"

Jack's chair squeaks forward as he rests his elbows. "…that you're here? What, and spoil the surprise?" He presses his lips into that "duh" expression people use when they've said something obvious.

"C'mon, Jack. Out with it."

He huffs out a sigh. "Just let it go. Okay?"

"Yep. Right after you tell me what I did wrong."

He shakes his head. Sighs again. "Not you. Me. I used to…never mind. Ages ago." He tosses a hand. "I'm a happily married man. Very happily married. But still, I shouldn't have…"

"You shouldn't have let me stay here."

Most likely, Dobbs started it. One pseudo joke would have been enough. I hear it in my imagination. "You see that piece of ass sleeping in Jack's office?" The innuendo would have spread through the whole department like a gasoline fire, rising from the coals of Jack's profligate youth to incinerate his reputation all over again and undermine his authority inside of a minute.

I copy his sigh. "Does your wife know I stayed here?"

During the glum silence that follows, another intuitive certainty takes hold.

"You told her."

I shut my eyes tight for a second. "You nice, nice man," I scold. "You nice, stupid man."

I hastily collect my laundry and purse, which contains my car keys and the Glock, and finally the McDonald's bag. Backing out the door with my arms loaded, I assure Jack Jenkins I am getting out of his life and getting on with mine.

"Promise?"

"Promise. My shadow will never again darken your door."

Jack's impish smile isn't especially convincing. "From your mouth to God's ears," he says by way of goodbye.

The Jeep is sitting exactly where I parked it when I first arrived. The spare key is on the driver's seat.

I consume the lukewarm McMuffin in the police station parking lot. The coffee I sip at stop signs and traffic lights. I drive slowly through the suburbs of Albuquerque, savoring the anticipation of seeing my father, but also admiring the homey neighborhoods, the strip malls, the greenery—or lack thereof. The mountains. The purity of the light. The populace. The smell of the air.

In the morning sunshine Dad and Ana's home radiates warmth. I would like to say the one belonging to the woman who reported me to the police looks cold and gloomy, but that isn't true. All around me are neat yards. Cute mailboxes. Flowers blooming in September. This is an inviting, if modest, neighborhood. The sort where residents respect privacy, but also manage to look out for each other.

I leave the Jeep at the curb in its brilliant orange splendor and approach the blue door with the useless window.

My father answers my knock within seconds. His feet are bare, and he needs a shave. He's wearing a striped bathrobe I don't recognize and a dumbfounded expression.

Before I can even say, "Hi, Dad," he doubles over and stumbles back as if somebody sucker punched him. He coughs so hard he almost gags. With his right fist tight against his belly, his left hand claws empty air as if reaching for something to keep him upright. I think maybe he's having a heart attack.

"Dad...?"

In the short distance to the left a rectangular table is surrounded by rustic chairs. I slip past my father and drag one of them across the patterned tile floor and place it behind him.

He sinks onto it as if it's the last seat in a lifeboat.

I don't know where my father is in his head, but he isn't here with me.

"Dad? Dad! Are you alright?"

He lifts his chin to meet my eyes. His are pooled with tears.

"I thought you were..." He waves his head, snuffles into his sleeve.

"Who, Dad. Who did you think I was?"

He looks up again. "Ana. I thought you were Ana."

"Why?" Wouldn't his wife have her own key?

"She's gone," he tells me. "I can't find her, Beanie. I've looked everywhere."

Chapter 8

KELLY SETHI WAS BORED. It was a Teachers' In-Service day at her school, and although she was nine-and-a-half, her mother didn't feel comfortable leaving her for hours on end while she minded her shop. "You have a whole mall to explore," Mother explained. "Buy a book. Get a milkshake. Take a nap in the back…"

All of which Kelly had already done, and more.

The shop primarily sold imported fabric items from India—lush bold colors with patterns that gleamed temptingly off scarves and cushions. Sheer, machine-embroidered cotton tops and skirts for women, and girls, too. Small animal sculptures painted purple and red and orange sparkled with tiny fake jewels. The real jewels were reserved for the rings and bracelets made by Kelly's mother. Set in silver, of course, as gold was too pricey for Mother and her customers both.

Kelly was born in Colorado Springs, USA, a normal American girl with exceptionally black eyes that shone like onyx and beautiful wavy black hair only slightly less shiny. Kelly's mother brushed her waist-long locks every night and braided them every morning.

The straight-A student played field hockey in the fall, girls' basketball in the winter, and ran track in the spring. She was as fast a reader as she was a runner, and had recently decided to become a writer like J. K. Rowling. Book stores just for children would spring up from the popularity of her books. Adults would stand in line awaiting the release of her newest adventure story—for themselves to read, not just their kids. Mother would sell piles of them from her store, and fans would line up all around the vast oval of the mall to meet her and get her autograph.

Kelly's mother smiled encouragement every time her daughter gave her something new to read aloud to her father. It wasn't that her father couldn't read it himself. He simply enjoyed the ritual. And seeing his wife and daughter happy, too. He adored them, of course, and so he humored them.

"May I please walk Snoopy? Please, please, please?"

Mother was ringing up a customer, so she merely waved her head no.

Kelly knew there was more to fulfilling her parents' expectations than simply behaving well. Since both were successful immigrants, they set the bar of self-reliance— and courage—high.

Kelly approached her mother again when she didn't have a customer.

"Snoopy's probably even more bored than I am," the girl argued. "Plus, he probably has to go to the bathroom. Mrs. Brookhaven can't always take him. She works just as much as you do."

"Mrs. Brookhaven wouldn't keep a dog in her shop if she didn't have helpers to take him out once in a while. Anyhow, he's a grown-up dog so he probably doesn't need to go out as often as you think."

"But I've taken him out before..."

"Once, and you were gone too long. You scared me, Kelly. I even called your father."

"I was having fun. Was that so bad? Snoopy catches sticks, even when he's running away from them. You should watch sometime. He's really athletic." Her father admired good athletes, one of the reasons Kelly loved him and wanted to please him. Her mother read lots of books, but so did her English teacher. Sometimes her English teacher gave her the titles of books she should read next and sometimes even gave her the book.

Her mother's loving gaze suggested she was tempted to give in.

"Please? I'm really bored."

Her mother's expression eased into subtle regret. "It's too late, my sweet. It's already getting dark."

Guards were the reason Kelly was allowed to roam the mall, but not outside. Almost every thirty yards a retired man in a brown uniform was on the lookout for thieves. The brightly lighted employees' and shop owners' parking lot lay only slightly farther away than the guards stood apart. Also, Snoopy was a small, barky dog. Kelly trusted he would raise such a terrible racket if somebody scary came along that any nearby adult would certainly run to see what was wrong.

"But, but, but," she begged.

"No, Kelly. I prefer that you stay here."

Kelly clenched her teeth to hide her anger. Also, to keep from mentioning self-reliance and bravery. She might have to remind Mother about those qualities when she came back.

On her way to collect Snoopy, she failed to notice the man leaning against the white wall advertising a store that would soon be opening.

She did not see him push away from the wall and casually follow her to Mrs. Brookhaven's nail salon.

She did not see him wait for her to emerge with Snoopy on a short leash and head toward the mall exit leading to the employees' and owners' parking lot. Nor did she notice the slow smile that spread across the man's face when she and the dog turned down the narrow passageway to the seldom-used back door.

Forty-five minutes later, a woman returning to her car found Snoopy running wild in the parking lot. After capturing him by the leash, she called the number on his name tag.

Mrs. Brookhaven called security. Then she called the girl's mother.

The search for Kelly Sethi began.

Chapter 9

NOW THAT DAD and I have settled down at the kitchen table, I ask how long Ana's been gone.

"Three days," my father admits. Steaming mugs of coffee are within reach, but his hand is trembling too much to lift his.

"Have you notified the police?"

Dad shakes his head so hard some of his coffee sloshes onto the table. "She took her car and her purse, Beanie. Ana left on her own. So, no. No, I have not called the police."

"What about clothes?"

Dad shrugs. "I don't notice clothes. You should know that."

Trying not to seem rattled, I dab at the spill with a napkin. "Three days is a long time to wait. You want me to call?"

I begin to dig out my phone, but the panic on Dad's face makes me stop.

Something is wrong here…*but what?*

Ooooh…

My father is merely sixty-two, but he looks about seventy. Farming is tough outdoor labor, and brokering real estate is hard in its own way. Bernie Beck obviously gained weight since he gave up both, and his fine hair is more transparent than I remember.

I reach across the table to lightly tap his wrist, and his eyes shyly meet mine. "You're a super catch, Dad," I tell him truthfully. "You're the kindest, funniest, most loving man I know. I've never met Ana, but I know for a fact she would be an idiot to leave you. If the police can't find her, you and I will. Now start at the beginning. Exactly what happened?"

Dad's shoulders lower their grip, and he seems to breathe for the first time since he opened the door.

"I thought everything was okay," he relates with a flip of his hand. "Maybe she's been a little edgy, but who doesn't get that way now and then, right?"

He stares out the window. Waves his head to return to the present.

"I guess she was spending more time in her studio, too," he adds, then shifts his gaze down to the stove. "I'm learning to cook Mexican, can you believe it?" He huffs out a weak laugh, so I smile for a second, too.

"Her pottery studio?" I prompt.

"Yeah, in the back. I just went out for groceries," he ponders a moment, "and I probably took too long." Tempting displays are Bernie-Beck magnets.

"And when you got home?"

"No note. No nothing. I just had this bad feeling, you know?"

Dread. Yep. I knew it. "So, what did you do?"

"Put the groceries away. Started dinner. Hoped it was some sort of misunderstanding."

"And later?"

"I…I just didn't know what to do."

"You cry a little?" I smirk as if I'm teasing, but I'm trying to nudge him past the awkward bit.

He sneers at that, and we both laugh.

"What now, Beanie?" The nickname is short for Lauren Louise Beck, or L. L. Bean, the New England purveyor of clothes that almost never wear out.

"Now you're going to tell me exactly what you did so we can report it all to the police. Then we'll do whatever they either can't or won't."

I'm pleased to see Dad gazing at me the way he used to when I did something that made him proud.

"I'm glad you're here, Lauren," he admits. "But why on earth did you come?"

I shrug modestly, roll my eyes, and tell him I was hungry for enchiladas.

***

Turns out the morning after Ana disappeared, Dad phoned her three local girlfriends and asked if they knew where she might be. Each of them was as shocked and worried as he.

He also called the art studio that handles Ana's pottery, but the owner became so distraught he could scarcely talk. Apparently, Ana's work accounts for a large portion of the man's income.

"Did you approach any of your neighbors?"

Dad sips some of his cold coffee and slowly lowers the mug before answering.

"Millie, next door. Said she was aware of Ana leaving, but she didn't really see her go."

"No suitcase or box or anything?"

"Nah. Just heard the car."

"What kind of car?"

"A blue Chevy SUV. Usually parks on the curb, which annoys Millie because it's so big."

"Poor Millie."

"Yeh."

"Anybody else?"

"I tried Hazel over there," he gestures toward the other side, "but she didn't answer my knock. Pain in the ass, that one."

"This question is going to sound weird, but humor me."

"Okay."

"Does Ana look anything like me?"

Dad's eyes widen. "That's a serious question?"

"Yes."

My father waves his head. "Ana couldn't look less like you if she tried." He rises and heads around to the living room. Returns with a wedding photo in a silver frame.

Dark-haired with a beautiful olive complexion, Ana Beck appears to be younger than my father by a couple of decades. Her wedding dress was filmy white with red embroidery around the hem and is no less than a size 14. Ana appears genuinely happy in the photo. So does my father. Overjoyed, really. Both of them.

"I'm sorry I wasn't here," I remark. Actually, I wasn't invited. I don't know who was.

Dad looks even more melancholy. "Right after that crook pulled the rug right out from under you? Puh. Why spend all that airfare money for a fifteen-minute ceremony? You were here, Beanie." He holds a fist to his heart.

"You make a lovely couple," I remark.

"Yeh. Thanks," Dad responds without conviction. As if he's worried it's no longer true.

To divert him, I mention that I got mugged on his doorstep.

"What! When? Are you okay?" Dad rises half out of his chair as if he intends to defend me right on the spot.

I wave him back down. "I'm fine," I assure him. "It was just after twilight. Where were you, by the way?"

"Last night? In Mexico to see if Ana was with her sister. Marie doesn't have a phone."

"Who doesn't have a phone these days?" A stupid remark, which I realize immediately. Poor people don't have phones. Two months ago I could barely afford my own.

"Marie didn't know anything about Ana's disappearance?"

"You got that right. Please. Tell me what happened to you."

"I'm fine," I repeat. "The guy knocked me into your door, and your alarm went off. That's one hell of an alarm system, by the way. Was somebody else attacked?"

Dad's cheeks pink up, and he flips over a hand. "Nah, nothing like that. Ana's clay artwork. It's…it's expensive as all get out. She's pretty famous for it, Beanie. Seriously. They ran a big newspaper article about her a couple months back."

"Could that have anything to do with her disappearance?"

Dad decides that's unlikely.

Then he asks again if I'm okay.

"Fine, Dad. Let's check in with the neighbor across the street. Then we'll stop by the police station and file that missing person report."

Chapter 10

THE WOMAN ACROSS the street is named Janet, and when my father introduces us, neither she nor I mention last night.

"Lauren was a cop back in Landis, PA," Dad brags the way fathers do, "and if you don't mind, she'd like to ask you a few questions."

Janet raises her left eyebrow and looks me over for lice.

"I heard your alarm go off," she addresses my father. "Everything alright?"

"No," he answers. "My Ana is missing. We're wondering if you saw anything that might help us find her."

Janet blinks back and forth between Dad and me, finally settling on me. "Like what?"

"Did you see her leave? Notice any unusual vehicles lately? Anyone watching the house? Anything at all out of the ordinary?"

"Not really," she says, addressing my father. "A few weeks ago some young man knocked on your door so hard I thought he'd set the alarm off. But he didn't, so…"

"What did he look like?" I ask.

"Young. Dark hair."

Dad turns to me and shrugs. "Could have been Ana's son. We don't get many visitors." He seems apologetic, as if I might be disappointed their lifestyle isn't more interesting. Or else he's disappointed in his neighbor. Difficult to guess.

"Lauren was mugged out front last night. Did you at least see that?"

"Didn't look. I assumed *she*," snidely referring to me, "set off the alarm. She wanted to get inside bad enough."

Scarcely the wiser, we take our leave.

I offer to drive us to the police station, and Dad accepts.

"Her son?" I inquire as we climb into the Jeep. "Tell me about him."

"Haven't met him," Dad admits. "He's sort of in the wind. Pain-in-the-ass, if you ask me. Ana'd love to see more of him, but he never calls. Most of the time I don't think she even knows where he is."

I park a discreet distance from the entrance to the police station in the hope that Chief Jenkins won't walk past any front-facing windows for the next hour or so. Since by-the-book Sarge was night shift, I assume he's safely asleep at home, perhaps dreaming of handcuffing underage shoplifters. Since I am far from the only thirty-year-old blonde, it's unlikely anyone else will connect my presence to the rumor about Jack and me.

Dad and I approach the reception desk, and the officer manning it slides the bulletproof window aside so she can hear us. I explain who we are and that we need to report a missing person.

We are ushered into a room with multiple desks, less than half occupied. The officer we're introduced to is a veteran with hazel eyes that have seen pretty much everything. He has also lived some of what he's seen, because sorrow wrinkles appear when the duty officer explains why we're there. Officer Smith expresses sympathy. His actual name is Smith.

He snags a chair for me after Dad is settled down, and the interview begins. Smith asks good questions, the same ones I'd have asked. He dutifully photocopies the picture of Ana Dad brought along.

While Smith is outlining the usual procedures for missing persons, it happens, of course. Chief Jack Jenkins wanders in on some official mission and spots me from behind. Whereupon, he hastily winds through the desks in order to confirm the worst.

Yes, it's me.

His face frozen into a no-nonsense frown, he crooks his finger to get me off the chair and points to the way we came in.

I excuse myself and follow.

We arrive at a neutral zone with nothing but walls and closed doors around.

"What's up?" he demands. No doubt he noticed I was with an older man, so I assume he realizes something resembling actual police business is afoot.

"Is that guy a witness to your mugging, or what?"

"That's my dad. His wife is missing."

Jack strokes his chin with his thumb and forefinger while he cogitates a few chess moves ahead. "You think that's why you got mugged?"

"Gonna hafta get back to you on that," I admit. "The only motive I can imagine has to do with Ana making very, VERY expensive clay art."

"Ana Tomas?"

"I guess." I wasn't aware of her maiden name.

"Wow," Jack exclaims, and returns to playing mental chess. "Robbery, you think?"

"Doubtful. As I said last night, it felt like a potential abduction when it was happening. Maybe a prelude to rape."

"And I told you that didn't sound quite right."

"…because I just arrived in Albuquerque and hadn't even bought dinner yet. I know. The wrong place at the wrong time. But awfully random, I agree."

Jack sympathizes about my stepmother, the first time anybody has referenced Ana to me in that way. He promises he will personally keep tabs on the case and make certain my dad and I are kept up to date with everything they do.

"But you know the odds," he warns with gravity enough for a president's funeral.

"Yes." A lump in my throat prevents me from saying more.

Jack digs out a card and writes his personal cell phone number on it.

"You going to keep out of this?" He means am I going to investigate.

"It's my dad," I remind him. "But I won't interfere, if that's what you want to know."

Jack nods. Tells me, "Good luck," in a general enough way.

"Thanks again for the pizza, and the…the rest. I really…"

"Forget it," he says. "Please."

We each smile uncomfortably for a second.

"Your wife okay?"

"She will be," he says, his sideways glance demonstrating a little too perfectly how he plans to reassure his wife.

Chapter 11

ANGER COURSES THROUGH his veins like acid. Ducking under the overhang, he backs himself further into the shadows. Scans the illuminated patches of slanting rain for signs of movement. The clouds of his breath swiftly disappear in the wind.

A bag of food is warm against his leg, but it won't be warm for long. He hunkers down on the damp doorstep and eats like a feral animal.

It's her fault. He knows this as surely as he knows God made him the way he is for a reason, and he hates her for turning his life to shit.

Thinks maybe if he'd taken a little more time, he wouldn't have picked her, but thoughts like that just make him angrier.

He did everything to plan. Watched. Evaluated the risks. Chose a location. Watched that, too. So what if he was a little impatient? It was time. He was ready.

He decides maybe she was bad to begin with, the sort a father or brother or uncle would keep a close eye on.

Or another predator. Not impossible. She was a looker for her age.

She was good, too, just what he wanted…until she screamed and turned his life to shit.

He quickly shut her up, but not fast enough. Some wannabe hero heard her and came out of the weeds on the run.

No choice but to run himself.

And keep running.

He crumbles the food bag and curses.

Damned bad luck there wasn't time to kill the bitch proper. Aside from all that forensic crap they have now, they have her description of him. If he gets caught, her lineup I.D., too.

He's shivering. He needs to get moving.

No cars or trucks in sight. Not in this district at night. Maybe a watchman's vehicle parked outside his workplace, but only an idiot would hot-wire the ride of somebody ninety-percent guaranteed to be awake.

Returning to the burger joint for that Nissan was out of the question. He'd heard some cops have equipment to detect stolen plates almost instantly, and more shit luck, one had followed him into the burger joint to top off his coffee.

He decides maybe it's safe enough now. Okay to give some tired burger employee a bad surprise when he plods out to his car.

The rain lets up as he begins to walk, a good sign, but only for the present.

He'll need gas money for the long drive to his next location. Food. A warm, dry bed, and a shower. Clean clothes, too, enough to blend in.

Cash. It all takes cash.

The rain stops, and just as if God himself broke through the clouds, he knows exactly what to do next.

Chapter 12

"WHAT ABOUT KIDNAPPING?" I ask Dad as we pull away from the police station. "Do you and Ana have enough money to worry about that?"

Dad huffs out a snicker. "No, Beanie. You've seen our house. I drive an eight-year-old Ford…no."

"What about Ana? You say her art is really expensive. Any chance somebody thinks she's wealthy?"

"Art isn't groceries, Lauren. Anyway, she's just caught on. So, no. I don't think she would tempt a kidnapper."

"But you aren't sure?"

Dad sighs the way he always does when I won't drop a subject.

I pat his leg when it's clear he doesn't plan to answer. "Just checking. You'd probably have gotten a ransom call by now anyway." *Probably.*

Unfortunately, there are still high-profile kidnaps—mainly overseas—but there are also opportunistic, Hazel-ante kidnaps, some conducted on the phone and finished within minutes. I can't gauge whether Ana's recent fame makes her a target, but I know when times get tough enough, some people will risk anything to survive—including a prison sentence long enough to last the rest of their lives.

I'm happy to let my father be optimistic about not receiving a ransom call, but, in my experience, it's too early to rule anything out. For all I know, Ana could be a criminal herself, in some sort of unimaginable trouble.

I stop for a light. "How about your bank balances?"

If, as Dad fears, Ana left because she doesn't love him, she may have cleaned out their bank accounts on her way out the door.

Dad grunts and waves his head. "I checked yesterday. They look about the same."

"Credit cards?"

"No new transactions," he reports, as if that's a good thing.

Which it is not. That she's failed to charge a meal, or a hotel room, or even a coffee heightens the tension I'm feeling about all this. If Ana were on an innocent trip, why not tell Dad all about it? Or at least offer some innocent-sounding excuse?

The secrecy frightens me. It suggests too many unpleasant possibilities—one being Dad's main worry, but I'm not buying that yet. Not only did Ana leave behind a great guy, she also left the fully appointed studio where she created her art. Her livelihood, in other words. Were divorce her goal, she should have fessed up and negotiated to get the house. Just plain leaving made no sense.

Also, not touching joint finances may appear to be a kindness, but it also prevents her movements from being traced. Whether that's Ana's choice or someone else's remains to be seen.

"Does she have any accounts of her own?"

"Sure," Dad replies. "A business one."

"Direct me to your bank," I urge. "Maybe we'll learn something there."

***

The only bank employee with no customers at her desk appears to be sixteen, but is probably twenty-three. She has a narrow face, pointy nose, lank light brown hair so straight it looks ironed, and teeth just crooked enough to be cute. Her nameplate reads, "Sarah Brown." I want to call her Trixie just to spice her up a bit.

After introducing ourselves and shaking hands, we all sit down.

"We have a serious problem," I open, which flusters Trixie immediately. She blinks and lifts her hand as if ready for action, then drops it because her hand doesn't yet know what to do.

I tell her, "My father's wife is missing. The police are looking into her disappearance."

Trixie's face instantly reddens, suggesting either a sheltered life or a deep well of empathy.

"Can you please check her bank accounts for any unusual activity?"

Both Trixie and her hands are now happy. Armed with the pertinent details from Dad, she and her keyboard become one.

"Which account do you want to know about?"

"All of them," Dad and I respond in unison.

"I can't disclose information on her individual accounts. You know that, right?"

"Are they listed there?" Dad inquires.

Trixie purses her lips.

Dad rubs his chin. Gets a bright idea. Points an elbow at me. "She was a cop in Landis, Pennsylvania, you know." He says that with a solemn nod. "She's found missing persons before. Lots of times."

The young woman's brown eyes expand. "Really? You don't look...old enough."

"Thanks," I say with a neutral smile. *Neither do you...*

Dad digs a photo of me in uniform out of his wallet, and Sarah Brown's eyes grow larger.

"This is really quite serious, Sarah," I point out truthfully. "We don't know whether it's an abduction, a kidnapping…" I glance at my father, who has blanched, and decide to withhold the statistics on the tip of my tongue. I also delete the words *murder* and *rape* from the current sentence. "…or what's going on," I finish. "If we have to wait for the police to get a warrant, we'll waste precious time."

I needn't worry about frightening Sarah into cooperating. Her imagination is already there.

"What's on your screen, Sarah?" I prod. "Whatever you've got may help us bring her home safely."

I'm wondering whether the young bank employee noticed that my "us" bypassed the police. Nor did it include the FBI, whose purview, among many others, is kidnapping. So far there is nothing for the Feds to sink their teeth into. Of course, the second we do have something…

Sarah's quick glance encompasses the room, reminding me she may lose her job over what we're asking.

"She withdrew fifteen hundred dollars from her business account three days ago," Sarah recites just above a whisper.

Yay, Trixie, I'm thinking, as she takes in my proud smile.

"Thank you," I tell her with conviction.

"What else?"

Sarah peruses the screen again. "Just that she didn't take the cash out here."

Odd. "Where?"

She names a town, and my father tilts his head as if he's familiar with the place.

Sarah is really into it now. "Nothing from the Money Market account," she adds.

"What Money Market account?" Dad inquires.

Sarah pivots the screen toward us. Points. "*That* Money Market account. Notice the additions. Ms. Beck shifts ten percent of her earnings into it every time she deposits a check."

"Oh, yeah," Dad says. "I remember now. She's saving for her son's wedding present or some such. I forgot all about it."

I glance again at the balance. It looks as if Ana Tomas Beck plans to give her son a house.

"Does Julian have access…to, to this account?"

"No. Just her."

"No withdrawals?"

"Nope. Not ever."

That leaves the withdrawal from her business account, which was probably just traveling money.

Still, there are too many unanswered questions to allow for any relief on our end.

"May I give you my cell phone number?" I want Sarah Brown familiar with it just in case. Cooperative resources are gold in your pocket, even if you never need them again.

We thank Ms. Trixie and depart around 3:15 p.m. According to Dad, enough time to make it to the other branch before closing—not enough time to take him home first. He is knackered, as they say in the UK, ridden hard for the last few days, and it shows. For proof, he nods off in the car, and I have to stop and punch the address of the other bank into the Jeep's GPS.

I crack all the windows wide and leave Dad conked out in the passenger seat while I go inside.

Business is slow so near closing, so I'm able to show Ana's picture to the two tellers without waiting. "Do either of you remember her from earlier this week?"

The male teller glances at the woman teller and vice versa.

"I think I had her," says the man.

"I already know what transaction she made, so I'm not here to ask anything you can't, or shouldn't, answer. I just want to know if you remember her. And, if you do, how she behaved."

"Normal, I guess."

"Nothing odd about her at all?"

"Aside from her not using her regular branch? That was odd enough." He stops, waits for me.

"Was she alone?"

Another glance at the woman. "Yeah. Yeah. Alone," he confirms after getting the woman's approval. "A little rushed maybe. She was already gone before I realized she was in the paper a few Sundays ago. Really strange, what she does. I guess some people like it."

"Sure," I say, because what do I know?

So far, I know that the guy is a relatively new teller, and the woman seems to be doing a nice job breaking him in.

Regarding Ana? Nada.

"Nobody waiting for her outside?" I try, just to be thorough.

"Not that we could see, right?"

The woman nods. To be fair, they didn't have a view of the whole parking lot.

"But now you got me thinkin' of it," the man volunteers, "she didn't leave right away."

"What do you mean?"

"I saw her walk across the lot to her car, like fifteen minutes later after she left here. By then I'd put her together with the article in the paper."

"What direction was she walking?"

"Left to right past the door." The only way that made sense, since that's toward the main part of the parking lot.

I express my gratitude for the information, wish him good luck with his new job, and take myself out of there.

To the left.

Where, four days ago, Ana Tomas Beck did something that took fifteen minutes.

Chapter 13

DAD ISN'T WORRYING about how long I spent in the bank—or anywhere else—because when I peek in the car he's still asleep, his chin slumped down to his chest. I'm pleased he's finally relaxed enough to get some rest, but I don't kid myself it will last. Each day Ana is gone will surely feel more permanent, exponentially more painful than the last.

I leave him in dreamland and follow a foot-worn path up the slight slope to the parking spaces above the bank property.

Five teenagers stand to the side of a Rite Aid pharmacy's sliding door. The boy leaning against the building is peeling open a Snickers bar, the girl sitting on the ledge at the bottom of the window sipping a soda in a recognizable red can.

The sunny September warmth has put a glow on their young cheeks, and I wish I could guarantee them many more years of relative innocence. Sadly, the world we live in doesn't coddle youthful innocence anymore, and at the moment I can't afford to either.

Since two long yellow school buses are stopped at the nearby traffic light, I assume the kids walked to the drug store from their high school. If I'm lucky, the after-school sugar-stop is routine.

I show them Ana's photo, ask if anyone noticed her four days ago.

No luck.

I sigh and glance around. See no other businesses of particular interest, just a chain grocery store across the busy four-lane, a narrow locksmith shop with two parking slots outside, a pair of gas stations opposite each other offering identical prices.

I think the fifteen minutes Ana spent here may mean nothing, that maybe she just needed Rolaids or aspirin and noticed the Rite Aid sign. Yet this is the last verified place she's been since she left home, so I step inside the drug store and get swallowed by the usual chill.

The aisles are like anywhere else, easy-to-reach shelves labeled with overhead black and white signs. Nothing in sight Ana couldn't get in any pharmacy anywhere.

I roam the makeup aisle, touch a bottle of sparkly green nail polish. Certainly not my style. Do I even have a style? I turn and wander through the shampoo section, past hair color, shaving cream…

Banking over here still didn't make sense. A teller who knew her wouldn't challenge what Ana was doing with her own money, while strangers would—and did— notice her newness and wonder why she came to them. So maybe she pretended to have another reason for coming here.

I move along. Turn a corner.

What if the money wasn't for her?

I try to picture her meeting someone, either inside or out, and handing the cash over right away.

Nope. Just like banks, drug stores have security cameras. If handing over $1500 was so hush hush, any one of a hundred thousand spots would have been better.

Forget the air conditioning; tension is prickling my arms, raising the hairs on the back on my neck. Ana was here. But why?

I stroll past the corn chips and candy, turn left toward the pharmacy counters, and there it is.

A Western Union counter. The agent wiping it with a disinfectant cloth is quite tall, probably about forty-five years of age, but he wears rimless glasses that make him look older.

"Hello," I say, and the clerk looks up hopefully. "I'm thinking of sending money to a friend…"

Wrong approach. Honesty really is the best policy.

Except for when it isn't.

"Allow me to start over. How does one send money to a friend?"

The agent's eagerness has lessened, but he obliges me.

"You open an account—either here or with the app—connect it to your bank account or give me cash, then tell me where you want the money sent." His voice is surprisingly deep and warm.

"To whom, you mean. Right?"

"Yes. You either send it to their bank account, which we verify, or specify they'll pick up cash at one of our locations."

"Cash. I'm going to send cash."

"Fine. You'll get an MTCN…"

"A what?"

"A tracking number, which you share with the recipient. They present an I.D. and the MTCN at one of our locations. Then they get the cash."

"Immediately?"

"Almost. There's a two hour wait for first-time transactions. And our branch needs to be open. Obviously."

"Sounds easy."

"Yep."

"How will I know when and where the money's picked up?"

"Email."

"Cool."

"Yes, it is. Do you want to open an account?"

I present him with Ana's picture. "Did this woman happen to send money to someone four days ago?"

"Who are you?"

"Her stepdaughter."

Clearly, my answer is not acceptable, nor should it have been. No company known for moving billions of dollars around the world could be expected to have anything to do with what appears to be a customer's personal soap opera.

Still, it doesn't hurt to try.

"This woman, my stepmother, is missing," I confide. "My father is extremely worried, so I'm trying to help him find her."

"So?"

"So, there's a possibility she's being extorted, or blackmailed. That's why we're worried."

"I'm sorry, but that has nothing to do with Western Union."

"True. But it would be most helpful if you could tell me where the money was sent."

"I don't see how. But that's not the point. Privacy is an important component of our business. I'm sure you can understand why."

I can. Fortunately, I know someone with enough clout to insist on an answer.

There are no longer any teenagers to bump into as I pace the sidewalk outside the Rite Aid. During the eternity it takes for Jack Jenkins to decide whether to answer my call, I picture him using the same pained expression I got when I tried to thank him for housing me overnight at the police station.

"You want to know whether Ana Tomas used Western Union to send fifteen hundred dollars to somebody four days ago, and, if so, who picked it up and where."

"Yes."

Jack thinks about it for a few agonizing moments before he agrees to try.

"Don't hold your breath," he warns.

"You'll text me one way or the other?"

"Sure. Is this what you meant by not interfering?"

"Anything new on your end?"

Stymied, we both hang up.

Chapter 14

DRIVING HOME, I TELL Dad about the Western Union possibility, finishing with, "The cop I met after I got mugged is looking into it."

Dad brightens for a moment, but soon returns to his melancholy thoughts. I'd love to reassure him somehow, but without evidence what would change? Traffic is picking up anyhow, so I give up on conversation.

By the time I slide the Jeep to the curb back at Dad's place, the neighbors' vehicles are tucked in like a flock of roosted pigeons. I note them from habit, also because of last night's mugging.

"Any chance I can stash my stuff inside somewhere?" I inquire. Cars loaded overnight are a petty thief's delight.

Dad blinks, as if returning from somewhere else. "Sure. Sure, Beanie. Should have thought of that myself."

Unfortunately, Ana's studio is the most likely space to store my clothes, my few framed photos, my personal files, and other essential junk.

"She's not using it," remains unspoken, except on her husband's forlorn face.

"You must be starving," I hint, because I am. "Why don't you make us something while I finish unloading? Show off your Mexican?"

He perks up just enough. "Good idea."

On one of my trips back and forth, opportunity knocks. The neighbor on the right Dad didn't yet speak to is tugging a trash can to the curb.

"Need any help?" I offer.

"Nah, I got it. You moving in?"

I laugh. "No. I'm Bernie's daughter. Just stashing my stuff out of temptation's way."

She nods and rests her fists on her hips.

I sit down my last bag, the duffle with the Glock in it, and walk over.

"Lauren Beck," I tell her as I stick out my hand.

Before grasping it, the woman wipes hers on an old skirt with pockets the size of napkins. Her face looks like pizza dough, her eyes hard as sapphire.

"Hazel Knickerbocker."

"Listen, uh, Hazel…You may be able to help us. Dad's a bit concerned about Ana. Did you notice anything odd lately?"

"Like that she left?"

"Yes, like that."

A corner of her lip lifts into a wry smile. "Tell him he'll get used to it."

Whereupon dad's neighbor begins to head for her door.

"Wait! Did you actually see Ana go?"

She halts mid-step and turns to face me. "I did. Why?"

"Was she alone?"

"Yes." A touch of impatience.

"Did she take anything with her?"

"You mean like a suitcase?"

Perceiving my concern, Hazel admits that, yes, Ana had a suitcase with her.

"What size?" I press. "Large? Small?"

She shrugs. "Medium, I guess. With wheels."

"Did she take anything else?"

"Her car?" Another wry smile.

"This is serious, Hazel. Ana hasn't been in touch, and my father's worried something may have happened to her. Anything you noticed might help. Did Ana seem happy? Sad? Angry? Could you tell?"

"I dunno. She was movin' too fast. Determined maybe."

"How about last night? I got mugged right over there, and the alarm went off. Did you see anything then?"

"I was out. Right out here, you say?"

"Yes. He was a big bruiser, too. You should be careful." Frightening her like that felt a little mean, but it was true. She should be careful.

Hazel shakes her head. Proceeds to her doorstep. Halts long enough to remark, "That sort of nonsense is why I got me a shotgun." She twists her doorknob, then glances back to say, "That and my ex…"

Then she enters her house and slams the door shut behind her.

Hazel Knickerbocker will be fine.

My dad, maybe not so much.

Over a fragrant dinner of chicken burritos, beans, and rice, I decide not to share Hazel's information about Ana's departure just yet. Why hurt the guy any sooner than I have to?

Instead, I ask why he chose New Mexico.

Dad's fork pauses before he looks me in the eye. "You know Corinne turned me down, right?"

Suddenly swallowing has become uncomfortable. "I thought it was the other way around."

Corinne was my former cancer counselor, landlady, and dear friend. I expected her to become my stepmother. Hoped, may be a better word. Her marriage to my father appeared to be a given, right up until it wasn't.

"You left," I remind him.

But then I catch on. He left everything he knew and cared for—because she turned him down.

Dad sees my confusion.

"She didn't want me to watch her suffer, Beanie. Or have to do what…"

"…what you did for me." I finish for him. The next bite of burrito takes extra effort to get down, and another bite is out of the question.

Dad reaches across the table to grasp my hand. "You know I was glad to do it, Lauren. I'd do it again, too. For you. Or for Corrine. For Ana. For anybody I love."

He returns to his food, showing me the top of his head as he eats. It is freckled and scantly covered with fine, silvering blond hair.

I want to touch the freckles and stroke his stubbled cheek with my fingers. I would also do for him what he did for me—nurse him through whatever hell comes his way. Right now, that means making sure Ana's leaving was indeed her choice, and that she's safe.

The house phone rings, and Dad bolts upright. Lunges across the room. Presses the instrument to his ear. He's seen the caller's number. It isn't Ana.

"Yes?" he says, as if braced for a ransom demand.

A moment later my father's body twists and slumps against the table that holds the phone. His head hangs. He mumbles answers to what can only be one of the friends he phoned before he drove to Mexico. "No word," he answers. "No, no. Don't bother. My daughter's here…Yes, thanks for checking in."

After dinner, Dad begs off just after making up the sofa-bed in his and Ana's office and handing me a clean washcloth and towel.

I hug him and tell him we'll find her, tell him whatever the reason she left, we'll get to the bottom of it, "Together."

He nods as if he recognizes a hollow promise when he hears one.

Later, when I'm tucking myself in and turning out my own light, I think of the Maryland restaurant where I worked while living with my brother—the loud, jolly owner, the bar regulars. Comforting memories to help me sleep?

Useless.

I'm awake because I sense that my sweet, read-me-like-a-book father hasn't told me everything…and because of that seemingly pointless mugging.

I also fear that Ana Tomas Beck is in danger, and I can't even guess why.

I hate when that happens.

I really, really hate that.

Chapter 15

I WAKE UP YAWNING and stretching just after dawn, disoriented but eager. Crisp daylight seeps through thin drapes, revealing my surroundings to be Dad and Ana's office/guest room. Coming from nearby, my father's familiar snore takes me back to my childhood.

The pleasant memory disappears the instant I'm fully alert. Dad's new wife is missing, and it's my problem—and privilege—to solve. Yet I see no clear way to begin without Jack Jenkins's help. Getting the details of Ana's Western Union transaction may take hours or even days, which means I might as well go for a run. I've been crammed into a car too long. I need to move.

Leaving Dad to his blissful rest, I pad around to where my clothes are, Ana's studio, a moderately large space on the back left rear of the one-story bungalow. Through the wall of windows lies a patio with a view of distant mountains, and I step outside to drink it all in. Overhead, mature vines weave through a pergola and cast long lacy shadows across the cool bricks under my feet. I've begun to appreciate the appeal.

While digging my athletic gear out of the duffel, I consider carrying some sort of protection, but what? Running shorts don't exactly lend themselves to concealing a Glock. Instead, I settle on the pen knife from my key chain, wrap it in a tissue and tuck it into the cleavage of my sports bra.

Enjoying the peaceful time of day, I loosen up and head toward the mountains. Again, unlike Pennsylvania's gentle sunrise, New Mexico's morning light seems exceptionally clear and bright.

Dad's street soon gives way to fairly empty road. As I pick up speed, I choose another that appears to offer an even greater stretch of open space.

About fifteen minutes in, I'm on a two-lane strip with white passing marks that seem to point straight at the horizon. It's still quite early, and, with scarcely any oncoming traffic, the few vehicles coming up from behind easily swerve past.

Lucky, because the gutter to my right is a dangerously deep, grassy ditch edging rough, barren land sparsely dotted with weeds. Yet when a tanker startles me with a warning toot of his air-horn, I know it's time to turn around. Just a couple more steps…

Hearing the rev of another engine behind me, I risk a backward glance. Coming on fast is a dark pickup with a massive steel grille.

Oncoming traffic is nonexistent. I'm the tallest thing in sight. And yet the driver is flooring it. Aiming straight at me, apparently with no intention of swerving.

I dive over the ditch just in time. My knees and feet land hard. My head snaps against my arm. My lungs deflate in one big whoof. My arms and hands feel as if they've been sanded.

I raise up on an elbow to see if the driver had a clue.

The pickup is already far gone.

I lie back on the gritty dirt to recover from the shock. Off to the east, the risen sun glows like a gigantic spotlight. I shield my eyes and huff out a short laugh.

A pen knife. What was I thinking?

What lingers are serious questions. Was the driver half asleep? On something? Just plain oblivious?

Or did he intend to run me down?

It felt as if he did.

"What happened?" my father exclaims from the kitchen. "You're all scraped up."

"No worries. I just chose the wrong direction to run. Can breakfast wait until I clean up?" By the delicious smells, he's made coffee, pancakes, and bacon.

"Sure. Sure. Bandages in the sink drawer. Help yourself."

My arms are bleeding a bit, and also a knee.

I carry some clothes into the bathroom with me, luxuriate in the shower until every trace of dirt and grit are gone.

Wrapped in a fluffy pink towel, I open the sink's top left drawer. Clearly Ana's domain, there are tweezers and a nail file, a jar of cotton balls, a smear of blusher dust, and one lipstick. It seems that Dad's new wife prefers the natural look.

I find what I need and tend to my scratched arms and knee. Then I dress in lightweight jeans and a t-shirt. White sneakers, and I'm ready to go. In this climate my long hair will be dry in minutes.

I wait until my last bite of pancake to ask Dad whether Ana is a "girly girl," or whether she's more like me.

My father was clearing the table, and he turns from the dishwasher to laugh at my question.

"She likes clothes, I guess."

"Yeah, but what about makeup? Is that an everyday thing, or just for a special occasion?"

Eyebrow arched, Dad lowers a plate to the rack before facing me front on. "You're not just making conversation, are you?"

I fold my arms and lean back against my chair. "Answer my question first."

Dad breathes out a wistful sigh. "Ana won't go anywhere without mascara and all that other stuff she uses. Okay?" He meets my gaze. "Your turn."

I nod and gently rest my bruised elbows on the table.

"Since Ana's mascara and 'other stuff' aren't here, I think we can assume she took it all with her."

"Yeah, so?"

"So, it's unlikely a kidnapper would wait for a victim to pack her toiletries. In other words, I think you can stop expecting a ransom demand."

Since my father exhibits no sign of relief, I remember that kidnapping isn't his personal fear.

Which tells me it's as good a time as any to mention that Hazel next-door saw Ana leave alone.

"So, I'm right," he says, waving his head as if it weighs a ton.

I don't want Dad dwelling on the idea that Ana may have wanted to look her best for someone else when we know so little about what's going on.

"Maybe not," I argue. "We'll know more when Jack Jenkins calls."

While my father busies himself doing some laundry, I snitch a sandwich bag from the kitchen and slip back into the bathroom. There I collect a few long dark hairs from the drawer where Ana must have kept her brush. A former-cop precaution, which may become useful if worse turns into worst.

At 10:49 a.m., Jack Jenkins's text interrupts Dad and me nursing coffees and trading sections of the Albuquerque newspaper. The text contains a dollar amount, a location, and a person's name. Busy guy, Jack Jenkins.

I reply using my phone's helpful "Thanks," suggestion, because now I'm in a hurry, too.

"Road trip, Dad," I announce. "Pack what you need for a couple days. We're getting out of here."

Chapter 16

WITHIN HALF AN HOUR Bernie and I are speeding north on a four-lane highway headed for a small town in Rio Arriba County. The traffic is ordinary for midday on an interstate, but the terrain is completely new. Equally beautiful and bleak, it is rocky and unforgiving, the colors either vivid or dull. I can't help but think, "cowboy movie."

Dad seems both eager and anxious, certain Ana will be there when we arrive, uncertain about the reception he'll get. After five days of unrelenting tension, I figure he's entitled to grasp at whatever straw he likes.

We've just passed by the edge of Santa Fe National Forest, and between the hum of the road and the wind rattling the ragtop, talking is a challenge. Still, why waste an opportunity?

"Tell me about Ana's son," I urge just short of a shout.

"You realize I never met the kid, right?" my father replies at equal volume.

"Whatever you got, Dad."

"One thing I know."

"Yeah?"

"I'd like to wrap my fingers around the ungrateful bastard's skinny little throat."

"Oh? Why?"

"Because he treats his mother like shit."

I pass an eighteen-wheeler. Then I ask if the kid is actually skinny or just young.

"He's nineteen," Dad replies with a crooked smile, "and he's scrawny. I saw a picture."

"What else?"

"He never had friends. Then in high school he suddenly did."

Traffic finally slows to accommodate a group of buildings—and conversation.

"You think he started dealing?"

"Probably marijuana. Maybe something else, I don't know. Ana says he earned enough working parttime at a gas station to buy an old van. Proud as hell of it. I dunno. My vote is drugs. Anyway, she almost never sees him."

We pass a road sign alerting drivers to Merriweather, New Mexico, which sounds familiar, I'm not sure why.

"You think Ana has any idea what Julian's been up to?"

"Hard to say. It's her kid, ya know? We kid ourselves sometimes, if you know what I mean. I know she checks her phone about ten times a day to see if he's been in touch."

As the offshoot to Merriweather zips by, I finally make the connection. It was in the morning's news, the home of another missing girl.

Traffic slows again for a stretch studded with traffic lights bracketed by large and small stores. We can read restaurant signs and see women pushing loaded grocery carts toward their cars.

Dad continues. "Once when I caught Ana crying, she told me how much she misses the kid. Sad for her, but also understandable. They were together more than half her life."

"How so?" I glance over and catch my father waving his head.

"She was only sixteen when she had him."

I do the math. Ana is only five years older than I am.

My brain fast-forwards to Ana's recent years. "Was she ever married, I mean before now?"

"Yes..." Dad nods for emphasis, "...to some terminally ill guy. He got free nursing. She got citizenship."

"Terminally ill," I repeat. "As in the guy died."

"Oh, yes. Years ago."

"Leave her anything?"

"No. What there was, he left to his boyfriend."

Ouch. "How did she manage?"

"The usual," Dad answers at a normal volume. "Worked her ass off to support herself and Julian. Did laundry, cleaned hotel rooms nights and weekends. Started baking wedding cakes for friends, and made a side business out of that."

"What about her clay artwork?"

"That's more recent. She took classes. Experimented. Her instructor let her use the classroom equipment until she could afford her own. Then she got an agent, good gallery support, a couple big commissions."

"What about the newspaper spread?"

"Yeah. That was huge for her. The icing on the cake."

I imagine Julian learning about the article and making hay with the information. Probably hitting up his mother for money soon after. Then, just this week, for fifteen hundred dollars.

Which, for a young man not long out of high school, is not just pocket change. It sounds like get-me-out-of-trouble money. How much trouble, and how much more money it requires, remains to be seen.

***

We stop for lunch at a roadside truck stop with several parked vehicles vouching for its food. It smells of warm bread and cinnamon. We are directed to a table for four next to a window with a view of the highway.

Dad chooses the ham platter with mashed potatoes, candied carrots, and apple sauce. He eats without his usual gusto, mechanically. But he eats.

I order three tacos with black beans on the side, partly because I ran this morning and partly because the price is right. All I know about Dad's financial situation is that he sold the family homestead to pay my medical bills, then attempted to sell off other peoples' farms into cookie-cutter developments. He obviously had enough to retire modestly and remarry. Yet, Ana's success as a clay artist aside, I have no idea whether Dad can afford this trip any better than I can.

The place has become quite busy, so while we wait on the check, I try a little nostalgia.

"Remember when you made oatmeal cookies without the oatmeal?" I prompt. Then, "What about when I called you a mess, 'M-A-S-S mess'? I must have been about five."

Dad smiles tolerantly—but chooses not to respond.

Wrong time? Or wrong approach?

Ana's disappearance has already bound us together, perhaps tighter than ever. So maybe now I can broach the subject that's been taboo between us for as long as I can remember.

I ask my father what my mother was really like.

Dad glances up from his food. Tilts his head slightly.

"Tall and blonde," he answers impatiently. "You've seen the pictures."

I have not. To my knowledge, there are none.

"C'mon," I coax. "I was seven when she died, and now I'm not. Do I look like her?"

Dad does that waffling motion with his hand. "You're taller. Similar hair color."

His stinginess annoys me, so I zero in on the tough one.

"Did we have the same kind of cancer?"

"No," Dad responds, his hazel eyes looking both hurt and hard.

The waiter rushes over with an apology and the check, and my father appears to welcome the interruption. I have no choice but to let the subject drop.

"Let me contribute," I offer, as he reaches for the bill.

"No thanks, Beanie," he replies. "This trip's on me." He slides a Visa out of his wallet, the sort held by a longtime card holder who pays on time. I expect it will appear again and again, whether he can afford supporting us or not. Nevertheless, I am relieved, and my father knows me well enough to know it.

I smile my gratitude and promise I won't order any filet mignon.

"Me either," he replies, the left side of his lip lifting into the familiar half smile of the father I love.

We sound like us again.

For now, that'll have to do.

Chapter 17

THE FIRST TIME was in early June. Ana had just cleaned up the remnants of her lunch and intended to return to her studio. An elaborate piece ordered by a wealthy patron was finally finished. She was eager to make delivery arrangements.

When she collected her cell phone from the sideboard, it startled her by ringing in her hand.

"Ma, I'm here."

After all the times she rushed to answer robocalls, checked and rechecked texts and emails, the shock of hearing her son's voice made Ana's body feel hollow, her bones fragile as straw. Half believing someone was playing a cruel joke, she made her way to the front door. Opened it a crack, then threw it wide.

"Julian!" She ran to embrace him, her loose sleeves flapping around his shoulders.

"Hey, hey, hey," he objected, wriggling away and stepping back.

Dismayed to see his weight loss, his limp clothes, his pallor, she, too, drew back. The desire to ask what was wrong nearly overpowered her, but such questions always sent him running.

"Why didn't you just knock?" she wondered aloud instead. "You know you're always welcome here."

Julian's wince at the mere hint of familiarity gave Ana a frisson of dread.

"Where's that man?" he inquired, glancing over her shoulder.

"Bernie is not home, but I know you would like him, Julie. He's your stepfather now."

Scarcely listening, her son rubbed his fingers together as if they itched. Patted his pant legs. "Can I come in, or what?"

"Of course. Of course."

As the door closed behind him, Julian bent forward, either with relief or exhaustion. Ana thought perhaps both?

"You hungry?" As a growing boy, heaping plates of food usually relaxed her son enough to be civil toward her. At the moment, she wished he would open up and give her a taste of what she so desperately craved—something, *anything,* about the missing months and years of his life.

"Naw. I can't stay."

Her hopes already dashed, Ana snapped, "Then why did you come?"

Julian's fidgeting escalated to a dance of swinging arms and restless feet. Risking one cautious glance at his mother's face, he admitted he was in trouble.

"You're on drugs." He had been before. Why should now be any different?

"No, Ma. Nothing like that. I just need to...to go somewhere for a while."

"You are running from the police?" Ana felt swollen, her body as ponderous as Buddha.

Julian drew his toe across the patterned floor tile. "Not the police," he almost whispered.

Eyes never leaving her son, Ana Tomas Beck hugged her arms tight against her chest and paced as if the chill she felt was real. Toughened by years of her own hardship, she believed her son when he said he was in trouble, but anything else out of his mouth would be a lie. He was here for money. It was as simple as that.

And if he got it, he would be gone, this time maybe forever.

Ana breathed in the look of the young man her son had become, memorized the way his ears peeked out from the waves of dark, uncut hair. The tilt of his nose. The sparse stubble on his cheeks. The familiar shape of his hands. And his eyes, the pupils as deep as a cavern.

What were his days like? His nights? Did he still work in a car repair shop? Did he work at all? Or was he too busy breaking the law?

"Sit," she said. "I have some paella. Left over, but…"

Julian sniffed at the motherly order, yet he pulled out a kitchen chair and used it. While he waited for the paella to heat, he contained whatever was going on inside his unkempt head with his two bony hands.

"You're too thin," Ana remarked as she scooped a sizeable portion of food onto a plate.

"You're not," Julian returned, and Ana caught what she thought was a smile as he picked up a fork.

When the plate was empty, Ana cut to the chase. "How much do you need?"

Julian pushed back from the table. "How much you got?"

The shift in Ana's perception came so suddenly it raised goose-flesh on her arms. For her dear boy, the child she'd raised to a young man, had fallen into an ugly repose, exposing himself to her just as she wanted, with an outcome no mother would wish. Her selfish, ungrateful child had become a callous, greedy adult.

Yet what could she have done differently? Much of her life had been hell, and if Julian felt put-upon and deprived, at that time there was nothing she could do about it. They were fed and alive, and for long periods it was miraculous she could manage that much.

Yet through it all, she loved her son without wavering, from birth to this very minute. He was all she had for so long—and she all he had. If a little bit of money was what it took for her to see him now and then, it was a price she was willing to pay.

Within reason.

"Got any cash?" If Julian had been assessing her as closely as she had been assessing him, surely he saw love and compassion.

Neither could he fail to notice her strength. Having a son at sixteen may have forced Ana Tomas to grow up hard and fast, but her recent marriage—and the resulting financial security—seemed to have fostered a confidence Julian could not have predicted.

Ana retrieved her purse from the front doorway. Fingering some bills out of her wallet, she placed them on the table in front of her son.

"I need it all, Ma."

Ana placed the rest of the bills on top of the pile.

"You'll pay me back?"

Julian's lips twitched. "Yeah, yeah. Sure, Ma. Every cent."

Chapter 18

AS DAD AND I leave the diner, my bandaged knee rubs against my jeans and reminds me of my nose dive into the dirt. It also reminds me to glance around the parking lot.

Of the assorted vehicles, three are pickup trucks. One is fire engine red and polished with pride. Two are dusty and dented from use. I haven't a clue what was on the morning's license plate, but I memorize numbers of the two dusty ones anyhow. Then I stroll around to check their front.

Maybe. Maybe not, regarding the grilles. In Dad's semi-rural area there are probably enough well-used pickups to double stack a very large junkyard. It may be a stretch to think we're being followed. But if we are, it can only have something to do with Ana. Precautions are surely in order.

Only minutes past the truck stop, Dad and I near the town with the Western Union where Ana may have gone, and we fall silent to listen to the GPS's instructions.

This Western Union proves to be another booth inside a drug store, and the female clerk seems amenable enough when I explain.

"I do remember your wife," she tells Dad with sympathy. "She was really upset that she missed her son. But to be honest, she should have known better. It just takes a couple hours to deliver the first transaction."

"You're sure it was her son who collected the money?"

"He showed valid I.D., and he had dark hair like hers. Anyway, she convinced me it was her son. She seemed desperate to see him."

Beside me, my father stiffens, and his personal pain gives me pause. Yet this is our only lead. I need to get as much out of this clerk as she's willing to give.

"You can make fifteen hundred dollars available that fast?" I press.

"No…" The woman looks a bit flustered. "Not quite that much."

I start guessing numbers, "Fourteen hundred?"

No reaction. "Thirteen hundred?"

"Twelve hundred?"

The clerk watches me and waits.

When I get to a thousand, she lifts her chin and looks away. I've just *not* been told Julian only picked up a thousand dollars; which suggests Ana kept $500 of her withdrawal for her own use.

Logical, but also troubling. Dad checked multiple times, and Ana hasn't made any credit card transactions since she left.

Which means she's chosen to travel anonymously.

Further confirmation that her son isn't just late with his rent.

***

Out in the pickup-truck-free parking lot I tell my father I need to phone Jack Jenkins. Dad says he wants something at the drug store anyway.

It takes eleven rings, but Jack finally answers his personal cell. He sounds breathless. "What?" he asks abruptly.

I tell him I'm convinced Julian Tomas is on the run. "Former high school drug dealer, no known residence or occupation. He's also hitting up his mother for money from anonymous locations."

"I'll check into it," Jack agrees, "but you know what the odds are, right?"

I do. Unless Julian's crime took place in Jack's jurisdiction, or the kid is suspected of something already on the national radar, it's unlikely Jack will be able to pinpoint what Ana's son is running from.

"Just telling you why I'm more worried than before," I explain. "But there's something else, too."

"What?"

"A pickup almost hit me when I was out for a run." I describe where I was and the approximate time of day.

"That's a dangerous road for a runner anytime..." Jack begins.

"Yeah, but..."

"...you're not from here," he finishes. "You sure it was deliberate?"

"Pretty sure. He sped up when he saw me. Want me to send you pictures?"

"Of what?"

"My injuries. Cuts and scrapes. I had to dive..."

"No! No thanks."

"Okay, fine. But I did get mugged on my Dad's doorstep."

"Right," he concedes, "and I don't blame you for being a little paranoid. However, that event...those events...don't mean your stepmother didn't leave completely on her own. Sorry, Lauren. The woman probably doesn't want to be found."

"But Julian's been involved with drugs. What if he pissed off his dealer?"

"I'll be looking into that. But don't hold your breath."

I close my eyes to the breeze blowing trash across my foot. "Can you at least do me one more favor? Please? It's really important."

Jack sighs into my ear. "What?"

"Ask your source at Western Union to tell you if Ana sends Julian any more money? The point of all this is to make sure she's safe, and I've got a feeling she isn't."

"You've got a feeling..."

"I'm gonna send you those pictures. Maybe then..."

"Don't threaten me, Lauren Beck." There is humor in his voice, finally.

"Okay," he says.

I breathe again.

Chapter 19

THE WESTERN UNION clerk kindly directs Dad to a "reasonable" motel with the usual restaurants nearby. It is just what you'd expect, a squared off U shape with an overhang sheltering the doorways. Dad and I ask for side-by-side rooms, and the daytime manager obliges with two on the far end of the U. Only three other cars occupy other visitors' slots, which is understandable. The place isn't exactly the Hilton.

"What's in the bag?" I inquire, curious about what my father bought at the drug store.

He shoots me a dirty look, so I imagine anything from condoms to jock-itch powder.

"Sorrrreee," I tease with a smile. "Pretend I was eight years old for a second." Back when I was completely honest with him and believed him to be completely honest with me.

"You wish," he responds with a yawn, reminding me that worry is exhausting.

While Dad naps, I stroll around the motel looking for anything out of place. Then I watch a house-renovation show on TV, the equivalent of a nap for me.

Around seven, we drive across the four-lane highway to a restaurant with an incongruous Swiss chalet exterior and lots of cars in the lot. It's late-ish for Dad's dinner, super-late for me. Back in Maryland I used to eat before my evening bartending shift.

As if the hostess senses where I'll be most at home, she parks us at a table for four protruding from the wall nearest the bar. Many varieties of beer appear to be on tap. The wine list favors imports from Germany. I feel a bit as if I've been teleported into another dimension.

I order beer. Dad chooses a Margarita, which the waitress warns they make with beer. Dad doesn't care.

I ask him how he's holding up.

He closes his eyes, then tilts his head as if stumped for an answer.

"Never mind, Dad. I think I know."

He sends his gaze out the window into the hastening dark.

I reach across and stroke the fist he set on the table. "We'll find her, Dad. I promise."

"I believe you, Beanie. It's just…I need to know why, you know?"

Why she left without a word.

"She loves her son," I remind him.

Dad waves his head. "I hope he deserves it."

"Hey, you love me. Even when I ask questions like what you bought at the drug store."

He laughs. "That really is none of your business. But I guess you're right. Ana would love Julian even if he robbed a bank."

"What's Ana like?" I ask, hoping that isn't another touchy question.

"Sweet. Fun. Creative. Damaged," he answers with fondness in his voice.

"From her background," I surmise, referring to the damage.

"Yeh."

"Would you say she's worldly?" I'm wondering how savvy Ana would be in her quest to see Julian in person. Would she learn from her first mistake and allow time to intercept him at the next Western Union—assuming, of course, that Julian plans to ask for more?

"Absolutely," Dad answers without hesitation. "Ana has street smarts to spare."

She also has a mother's implacable devotion to her son.

The bartender brings our drinks personally, suggesting the place is understaffed. I smile up with appreciation—of him. Obviously athletic, I speculate that his day job is either moving furniture or felling tall trees. Wavy, blond hair, penetrating eyes. No wedding ring. I hold my stare until he smiles. Then I thank him nicely for delivering our drinks.

He turns to leave, but glances back. Hopefully, I hope.

After I finish watching him, I note my father's annoying smirk.

"None of your business," I remark, repeating his line.

"Not anymore," Dad concedes.

In truth, I have no idea what Dad knows about my once-and-done love-life. I like to think of my approach as expedient, Scarp being a temporary exception. If you can't have children and don't want to deprive your partner of the family experience, one solution is to not encourage attachments. Sure, I may settle down sometime. For companionship. For love, who knows? But I'm not sure who I am yet, and until I sort that out, I protect myself—both physically and emotionally.

"I'm having the Wienerschnitzel," Dad concludes, tapping the menu on the table.

"You know that's fried veal, right?"

"Yep. That's what I'm having."

I choose Sauerbraten, which requires beef brisket to be marinated four days and includes cabbage along with other vegetables. I assume the marinade preserves the beef. At least I hope it does.

When our dinners arrive, the fragrance almost makes me forget about the bartender.

After we've made a dent in our entrees, I address my father. "So, why does Hazel next door have such an attitude? She really seems to hate Ana." Hazel is the woman with the shotgun, as I recall.

My father is actually blushing. He holds his knife in one hand and fork in the other, and for a moment seems confused about what they're for. Eventually, he meets my eye.

"When I first moved in," he mumbles.

"What's that?"

Dad juts his chin forward and nearly shouts, "When I first moved in, she had a thing for me."

The woman eating four feet away snickers.

"You happy now?" My father's cheeks are an even brighter red.

"Not quite. How did she…did she manifest this *thing*, as you call it?"

Another mumble. "She baked."

"Speak up, Dad."

Another shout. "She BAKED for me. Every day another cake, another pie. I gained ten pounds."

"Never lost them, did you?"

Bernie Beck glares at me, his one and only daughter. "I'll have you know, Ana happens to be a very good cook."

"The way to a man's heart *attack* is…"

"Don't start," he warns, spearing a hunk of fried meat.

This is actually fun, this is getting to know my father again. The next smile I direct at the bartender is matched by a huge grin.

"Here. Taste this," I offer, holding out my plate.

"Lauren, stop," Dad insists, and the expression on his face sobers me instantly. "There's something you should know."

I set down my plate, rest my hands on the table, and wait.

When Dad looks up, my heart nearly bursts.

"Sex," he says. "Ana and me. It isn't good, Beanie. She's…she's reluctant. I don't know what I'm doing wrong. I try to be patient, gentle. I…I just can't seem to…to get it right." He is nearly teary now.

So am I.

"Dad," I implore. "Dad, I'm so sorry. I doubt it's you. Some women…" I stop talking, because what the hell do I know about Ana's sexuality, or my father's, for that matter. I just hate that he's blaming himself.

He swipes his nose with his hankie. Looks straight at me. "I think that might be why she left."

I want to erase his hurt, but I need more information. "You don't screw around, right?"

"No."

"Didn't have a big argument?"

"No. Nothing like that. I thought we were okay. Except for the bedroom, I mean. We…love each other. At least that's what I thought."

"Dad, you're loveable. Trust me, I know. Why would she marry you if she doesn't love you, too?"

"For security, Beanie. She did it before."

"Okay, maybe. But then why did she leave?"

"That's it, Beanie," Dad concludes. "That's what I need to know."

When we've finished our meal, I take our empty drink glasses over to the bar and set them down. Again, not what is usually done.

"When do you get off work?" I inquire.

"Restaurant closes at ten. Family crowd," the bartender explains with a soft smile. "Sean, by the way."

"Lauren," I reply.

"Maybe I'll see you later? Good beer," I conclude, tapping my empty glass with a fingernail.

Back at the motel, Dad excuses himself and retires to his room. Privacy. We're both more used to it than to so much togetherness. Also, today has given us both quite a lot to digest.

I noticed a pickup across the way when I parked. So, now that it's dark, I wander over to check the license plate. It doesn't match the two I memorized, but I'm only half relieved. Tense. I've been tense all day, I realize. Maybe another beer will help take off the edge.

It's 9:40, and with Dad's snore audible through the thin motel walls, I slip behind the wheel of the Jeep and sneak back across the street.

The beer tastes better this time, and I say so.

Sean smiles. He has a lovely, warm smile. Not beautiful. That I wouldn't like. But I would enjoy rubbing my thumb across his lips.

We talk while he washes glasses and generally putters around, closing up the way bartenders do. When I finish my drink, he wipes the counter without taking his eyes off me.

I haul my purse up to dig out what I owe for the beer, and the purse makes a loud clunk on the bar.

"What you got in there?" he asks. "Bricks?"

I've relaxed enough to admit it's a Glock.

"Whoa!" Sweet Lips exclaims. "What've you got that for?"

It's been a long day. A helluva long day, so rather than bother inventing a clever lie, I perform a little one-shoulder shrug and tell him the truth. "I think somebody tried to kill me this morning."

"No kidding. How?"

"Pickup truck sped up when he saw me. Had to belly-flop off the road." I show him the scrapes on my hands.

"Wow."

"Got mugged the other night, too."

The bartender spins around as if he can scarcely believe it…correction, can scarcely believe *me*.

"Wow. Fuck. Listen. I hope you don't mind, but I think I'll just go home when I'm done here."

Good boy. He has just imagined somebody bursting in on us, shooting me, and then him.

I admire his common sense.

Also, I really do need some sleep.

Chapter 20

AFTER I LEAVE the understandably cautious bartender and return to the motel, the pickup I checked earlier is no longer among the half dozen vehicles in the lot. Yet before I park, I drive around the back of the motel to see what's there.

Not much. Just a pair of dumpsters.

Rounding the end of the building, spotlights weakly illuminate the service station beyond the office. Through the skimpy pines edging the property, I see five vehicles left overnight, including one pickup. By now, all that remains of my mini beer-buzz is a yawn, so I remind myself that pickups need repair the same as anything else, and I really should turn in for the night.

Hopping out of the Jeep just outside my room, I smile briefly over the uselessness of locking anything with a ragtop. Keeping the Glock on the bedside table overnight makes much more sense.

Just as I flip on the room's light switch, the nearly closed door opens again.

I lurch forward, but not in time. The sleeves of the familiar canvas jacket encircle my chest. A rope tightens around my neck.

With all the force I can manage, I ram my elbow back into my attacker's stomach.

No relief.

Hugging my saddlebag purse close, I hook my foot behind the thug's knee and sweep us both to the floor. We land alongside the bed's short metal legs.

Desperately squirming, I arch back hard to slam my attacker's face with my skull.

The rope loosens slightly. No more.

Desperate for air, I fumble inside the purse with my right hand. Grasp the Glock's barrel. Tug the gun free. Strike my assailant's leg with the handgrip.

No effect.

The hand twisting the rope is pressed against the side of my neck. Taking what may be my last chance, I wallop it with all the strength I have left.

Finally, *finally,* a deep, guttural grunt tells me I've done damage.

When I strike again, the injured hand releases the rope.

I wriggle onto my back as quickly as I can and suck in precious air.

Still close—too close—my would-be killer cradles his broken hand. Three spatulate fingertips embedded with grime protrude at a disturbing angle.

Before he can gather himself, I free the safety on the Glock and aim at his chest.

The thug pushes himself upright. Struggles awkwardly to his feet.

I rise and back out of his reach. Through his stocking mask I see dark hair, a grizzled chin.

"Who are you?" I demand as he backs toward the door. "Take off the mask."

The thug exits so fast the door ricochets off the wall and crashes shut behind him.

I step outside in time to watch him climb into one of the nearby cars, fire it up, and roar away. The car was unremarkable. Just light colored and small. I'm still too dazed to catch the plate number.

I knock on Dad's door to check on him.

Sleep drugged and wearing threadbare pajamas he's owned for decades, he has never looked better.

"Whasup, Beanie?"

"Never mind, Dad. Go back to bed. It can wait until morning."

Chapter 21

JUST SO YOU KNOW, I couldn't shoot my attacker because I don't keep bullets in my Glock. Not to mention, if I killed the bastard, I wouldn't be free to find Ana.

Too bad, all of the above.

Now that I know my dad's safe, I walk to the office and confront the night clerk. Tell him I was ambushed as I entered my room. "Know anything about that?"

No need for him to actually say, "No." The guy's wispy moustache quivers over the horrified O of his mouth. He rubs his cheeks, blinks at the counter, and seems to wish I never crossed his threshold.

"Well, it happened," I point out to remind him I'm actually here, "and I'm not staying in that room tonight. How about giving me the extra key to my father's?"

Whiskers ignores me. The hand he holds waist high over the counter is shaking. "You callin' the cops? You call the cops and the owner will kill me. This place ain't doing so good, you know? Cops coming would hit the news and, and…"

…and the place would go under and this poor guy would be out of work.

I sympathized. The whole enterprise screamed, "Hard times." Also, I knew what the local cops would—or wouldn't—do with a claim by a transient woman who somehow managed to prevail over an attacker in a stocking mask. Not even a license plate to go on? Forgetaboutit.

"How about that key?"

"Why can't you just knock?" the clerk practically begs.

"Because my father sleeps like a rock," a slight exaggeration. I would rather not wake him again. "You got a fold-away bed?"

"No. And I dunno about the key. What if your dad don't want you in there?"

Sighing with frustration, I pull my collar aside to show him my neck.

"Shit. You musta really pissed somebody off."

I wait.

"Oh, alright." He hands me the spare key and tries to make his escape.

"One more thing," I call after him.

"What?" the guy grumbles as he turns around.

I dig Ana's picture out of my purse. "Has this woman stayed here recently?"

A cursory glance. A wave of the head. "I wouldn't tell you if she did. T'wouldn't be ethical."

"Shall I call the cops and ask them to ask you?"

The guy shoots me a glare, so I pull my collar aside again.

"Why you need to know?" he asks.

"She's missing."

He gives Ana's picture a closer look. "Naw. Haven't seen her."

"You're sure?"

"Yep. Positive. We don't get single women, 'cept maybe you."

"Okay, thanks."

"Can I go now? I gotta get off my feet."

Outside, the night is so still it feels like a movie set. This time, I pull my collar aside to let the air cool my neck while I stumble back to the opposite side of the U.

Both exhausted and wired, I collect what personal items I need from my room and deposit them in Dad's. Another trip for linens and pillows before I address my injuries with aspirin and a soothing shower. At last, I settle down on the floor. My father's rhythmic snoring isn't quite the comfort it used to be, but it'll do.

All things considered, when Dad wakes up, he's only slightly surprised to find me here.

"I'll explain at breakfast," I promise, and we go about our morning routines as if we've done it forever without interruption.

The diner down the road is almost finished fueling early blue-collar workers for their hard-working day. Judging by the laughter, a couple men in matching company jackets have been ribbing the youngest guy for leaving an extra-large tip. I catch the moon-faced waitress cleaning off their table smiling fondly at the retreating youth's ass.

Life goes on.

Dad and I choose a lonely spot against the wall that houses the rest rooms. What we have to discuss is nothing the young waitress needs to hear.

"What happened?" Dad asks, after she drops off menus and mugs of steaming coffee. He's seen my bruised neck. He can also see that I'm fine.

I tell him the truth.

His face flushes with contained anger as he voices his conclusion. "Ana's in trouble."

"Maybe, Dad," I concur. "But maybe not. That's what we're trying to find out."

"You get anything like this while you were driving here from Maryland?"

I admit I did not.

"And what else you got going on but Ana?"

There's no arguing with his reasoning, so I don't even try.

After we've placed our orders, I mention that I promised the night clerk not to report the attack, but I've changed my mind. "Okay if we drop by the police station before we head out?"

"Head out?" he exclaims. "To where? We don't have a clue where Ana is now."

He's right, of course. Unless Jack hears about another Western Union drop, we have no idea where to go next.

"Maybe I should take you home so you'll be there if Ana gets in touch. Then I'll…I'll just wait for…"

Frustration reignites Dad's anger. Stifling a loud outburst, he draws his hands into trembling fists. "Why…why can't she just call?"

Our food arrives, an excuse to sink deep into our private thoughts.

My father deals with the check again, while I google the address of the local police.

When we arrive at the station, he opts to wait in the Jeep. Safe enough considering where we are.

I deliver my report to a sturdy sergeant who pretty much admits what I already know. I've given him very little to go on.

"But I do appreciate you coming in," he concludes, as he escorts me back to the entrance. "The big picture, right?" If the whole Ana mess ever gets sorted out and some lawyer needs to connect the dots, this dot will be in place.

"Yes," I concede, but then I remember. "May I ask you about something else entirely?"

"Sure."

"The girl missing in Merriweather. Has she been found?"

"Afraid not," the sergeant admits. "Why are you interested?"

I admit I lost a child back on the job.

"Sorry," he says with an empathy born of experience. "Haunts you bad, don't it?"

I remark that there seem to be a lot of abductions going on. "Or is it just me?"

"They don't all end like yours," he reminds me. "Last week a little girl got lost walking to a birthday party, and some Good Samaritan returned her to her grandmother. Word is the father was so shaken he quit driving rigs to be around more for his daughter."

Figuring to start a good mental list to balance the bad, I ask the child's name.

"Louella something."

I'm relieved to know she's one of the lucky ninety-seven percent. But that doesn't mean three percent of all the missing children in the country aren't gravely at risk—or that forty percent of those, mostly girls, won't end up like the one I failed to save.

"Beating yourself up doesn't do any good," the sergeant adds. "They say talking it out with somebody lightens the load."

I wave my head, and he reads my mind.

"Not necessarily a professional," he quickly amends. "Just somebody who knows what it's like."

He raises finger. "Wait here."

When he returns a few minutes later, he hands me a neon-green Post-it. On it are a name, a phone number, and an address.

"Who is she?" I ask.

"Nurse I met on the job. Her daughter disappeared about four months ago. No other family. She said her friends are well-meaning, but she still feels like she's going it alone. Maybe talking to someone like you would be good for her—and you, too."

Judging by the address, she lives nearby.

"I may not go."

"Your choice. Good luck finding your stepmother," he calls after me.

I smile back at him, waving the bright green note like the treasure it just might be.

Chapter 22

BEFORE I GET to Dad and the Jeep—and before I lose my nerve—I try the number provided by the compassionate sergeant.

I catch Cheryl Anderson at home and hasten to explain how I got her number.

"I'm not a reporter, just somebody who would like to know more about your daughter."

Her hesitation tells me it's a no-go, and I can't say I blame her. But now my throat aches—mostly from the lump in it. When I try to get out of the conversation gracefully, I can't.

"Who are you again?"

"Lauren Beck," I repeat. "I know this sounds crazy, but it would mean a lot to me if I could stop by…to…to talk about your daughter."

Her second hesitation feels promising.

"Okay, I guess," Cheryl finally agrees. "How soon are you thinking?"

I mention where I am, and we agree on a ballpark time-of-arrival.

***

Initially, Dad is lukewarm about the side trip, but he grudgingly admits it beats twiddling our thumbs until Jack Jenkins gets back in touch.

During the twenty-minute drive southeast to Cheryl Anderson's house, my father appears to be brooding about his missing wife, visualizing everything from the bad to the worst. To distract him, I try broaching my personal agenda one more time.

"C'mon, Stingy," I coax. "Tell me something about my mother."

Dad stirs as if he's unwilling to return to the present. Or rather to the past, for my mother has been gone more than twenty years.

"Don't you have your own memories?"

"Not many." Her disappearing—seemingly overnight—tops my short list. She was sick, Dad explained. "In the hospital," he said. Yet, at seven your mother being erased from your life can't help but feel sudden. For a time, I also feared I was to blame.

"I don't know who she was." I try to explain. "I want to know what she was like as an adult. Funny? Creative? Happy? Unhappy?" Mostly, I'd like to know whether I'm anything like her.

Dad huffs out a sigh. Rests his elbow on the Jeep's armrest. Throws his hand up with exasperated resignation.

The Jeep's GPS guides us through a quiet suburbs while I wait.

"She was complicated. Okay?"

"Go on."

"I never...we...I'm not sure I really knew her myself."

"Really?" I had notions of them whispering sweet words to each other, holding hands in the dark, sauntering down the tractor lane past the cornfields. Already, the way I imagined my parents' marriage sounds wrong.

"Did you pick raspberries together?" I ask stupidly, since Dad seems loathe to say more.

He shoots me a look. "That's what you want to know?"

"Yes."

"Why?"

"Because I remember eating raspberries."

"No, we did not pick raspberries together. I usually brought them back in my hat."

A start, at last.

"I remember red nail polish, too."

Dad rubs his chin. "Yes, Nina was always…" Another stall.

"Girly?" I supply.

"Vain probably. She was beautiful, as you know, and she took good care of herself."

I'm still stuck on the nail polish, how impractical it must have been for a woman on a working farm.

"Did she help with the outside work at all?"

"No, Beanie. She did not. It was all she could do to put dinner on the table. Or lunch. Or breakfast, for that matter. Your mother was not an especially practical woman."

"Did you love her?" Not meaning to be so blunt, I give my dad a quick glance.

He seems to be contemplating the horizon, so I tell him he doesn't have to answer.

Ah, but he does. "I fell in love with her at first sight," he says after some consideration. "It was after we got married I realized I loved the illusion of her, not so much the actual person."

"I'm sorry," I say, just as impulsively as I'd asked if he loved her. "Would you have gotten a divorce if she hadn't gotten cancer?"

Our route transitions onto a highway while Dad contemplates.

"Probably not," he replies, surprising me again. "I guess I did love her. We just didn't have much in common."

"Am I like her?" There it was. The Question.

My insides feel like electrified gelatin. Yet I am driving, listening for the GPS instructions, glancing between Dad and the road, practically holding my breath.

Dad shifts toward me and says, "Stop the car."

We are going seventy miles an hour. There are no exits in sight, no restaurant/gas station stops ahead.

"Give me a minute," I stall, as my hands begin to tingle.

In the eternity that lasts two minutes, a maintenance area appears. I pull in and park close to the inner edge where a man might hop out to pee. There are trees and weeds, a sky above so blue it looks solid, cars zipping by so fast I wonder how I'll manage to pull back into the flow.

The traffic isn't why I'm afraid.

"Hey, Lauren," Dad says as he reaches to touch my knee. My lower lip trembles as I turn to face him. "How long have you been wondering whether you're like your mother?"

"Forever? I'm certainly not like you."

He snickers, because we both know I'm quite a lot like him. Forty percent, probably. It's the rest of me that's a big blank.

"I really didn't know her, and I want to know more. Was my mother a nice person?"

My dad turns to face the windshield, and his body shifts to accommodate the change. "You are nothing like her, Beanie. You don't have to wonder about that anymore."

I'm thinking, *Not good enough.* Not even close. Why couldn't he look at me while he answered my question? Could there be something about my mother he would rather not say?

Maybe.

But maybe that's how it should be.

I restart the Jeep. Put it in gear. Tell him, "No worries," as we begin to roll. "I don't need to know anymore."

I hear him breathe. Catch an almost imperceptible nod.

Cheryl Anderson's house sits on a short lane off a suburban residential street and appears to be much older than the surrounding neighborhood. It has a porch, for instance, and old casement windows. The roof is also slanted in four different directions, as if a farmer added space as he and his wife had more children. Overall, there is an inviting modesty to the place.

"You go in." Dad recommends. "I'll wait out here."

"You sure? This may take a while." The morning has warmed considerably, and noon is approaching.

"Take your time. I'll be fine."

I leave the key in the Jeep's ignition so he can help himself to air conditioning.

Cheryl greets me at the front door, invites me to join her in the kitchen. She has been chopping vegetables for soup, it seems, but brushes it all aside to make room for two cold glasses of sweet tea.

We settle into leather armchairs in the adjacent study, which smells of furniture polish and old books, plenty of which are shelved on two walls. Two windows and a door look out onto a back porch with a narrow yard beyond. When the farming ended, some heir must have sold off every useable inch to a developer.

"Was this a family property?"

"Why do you ask?"

"I grew up on a farm," I explain, "then my father became a realtor."

Cheryl tilts her head knowingly. She is a soft woman with pale, shoulder length hair. She eschews makeup and wears comfortable clothes—jeans with a cotton blouse. I already like her.

She sips her tea, sets the glass on a coaster on the table at her elbow.

"I don't think you're here to talk about real estate," she remarks with an encouraging smile.

I offer an encouraging smile in return. "I'm here to talk about whatever you want."

An eyebrow arches. "I'm not sure I understand."

I explain how I was with the Landis, Pennsylvania, police until I had to leave, "for medical reasons." I tell her that while I was on the job I worked a case similar to what she's experienced, and I promised myself one day I'd get back in touch with the family of a certain girl I...

My throat catches when I get that far.

"...lost," Cheryl finishes for me, then looks away to swallow her tears.

"Yes."

She dabs her eyes with a tissue. "Why?"

"I wanted them to know that we...the police...will never forget them. That it may feel as if we're just doing a job, but we're human, too, and...and..."

"Yes, but why are you *here*?"

"The family in Pennsylvania moved away," I begin, but Cheryl has no patience for that.

"So...?"

"My father's experiencing something similar. His wife...his wife is missing. We've been looking for her together, but I keep coming across news about missing girls, and that reminded me of..." I can't go there, so I say, "I've been feeling this...this need to be with someone who..."

"Who's been through what you have?"

I sigh, and the lump in my throat eases slightly. "Yes, but I don't want release for me, so much as..."

"…for me."

"Yes."

Our eyes meet, and it's there. The understanding I've been craving.

My phone dings, alerting me to a text.

"My father," I remark to excuse the interruption. "He'll be back in half an hour. He went into town to get us some lunch."

Knowing the unpleasant details will come out on their own, I ask Cheryl to describe her daughter. Not necessarily what happened, just things parents like to brag about.

Four months ago, Lisa Anderson was a tall, lanky thirteen-year-old with long red hair and freckles. Eager for a vacation, her parents rented an RV and drove up to Yellowstone National Park.

"Lisa wanted to be a large mammal vet, so she was thrilled to see herds of buffalo. Three elk even crossed the path right in front of us."

Describing the Anderson's second night brought on Cheryl's tears. Knowing the campsite office sold necessities and snacks, Lisa took a flashlight and set off to buy a Hershey's bar.

The clerk on duty is on record saying she never arrived.

I try to picture the famous national park four months ago. Schools closed. Kids bursting with summertime freedom. Families itching to do something memorable. "Let's go see Old Faithful." Surely there are security videos, but what good are they with a humongous crowd? Even RV campground cameras couldn't be expected to cover the whole property, and Lisa's flashlight suggests large patches of darkness surrounding the sleeping guests.

I encourage Cheryl to relate happier stories, pets they had, other vacations, what subjects her daughter aced in school. The conversation seemed to cheer and relax the bereft mother, exactly as I hoped.

It also emerged that after the abduction, Cheryl's husband became, "bitter and angry, dissatisfied with everything." He finally moved out, taking their dog with him.

"Get another?" I suggest.

"Dog?"

"Maybe a cat?"

Cheryl laughs at that, a sound that delights us both.

"Stay for lunch?" she offers when our conversation finally lags.

"Oh! My father…"

I hustle out of my seat to check the driveway.

No Jeep.

My pulse skyrockets. My palms begin to sweat.

As if my face hasn't alerted Cheryl already, I announce that something's wrong. "Dad said he'd be half an hour."

She and I have talked at least an hour and a half.

I check my phone for any sort of message. Shut my eyes and scarcely breathe when there's nothing there.

"I'll phone the police station," Cheryl states as she rises from her chair. "They'll know about anything that just happened."

"Bernie Beck." I recite Dad's home address. "He'd be driving an orange Jeep."

Cheryl ducks around a corner to make the call out of my hearing.

By the time she returns several minutes later, I am terrified.

"Grab your purse," she orders in a take-charge voice. "Your father's in the hospital. They say he'll be okay, but he's already in surgery." She grabs her own purse, digs out car keys, and holds the front door open for me.

"What...what happened?"

The answer stops me cold.

"Not a car accident. Nothing like that. It was a drive-by shooting."

Chapter 23

CHERYL WIELDS HER little white Ford through the neighborhood toward the hospital with expertise. I'm grateful for this competent woman, fortunate to have been with her when I found out my father was shot. Her down-to-earth practicality is keeping my panic at bay, allowing me to close my eyes and let my thoughts and emotions run amok.

Shot and presently in surgery, they say regarding my father. And like it or not, there's not one thing that will relieve my anxiety until I get to the hospital and meet with his doctor. Part of me wants to scream with frustration.

Cheryl stops the car at the Emergency entrance.

Already grateful beyond words, I hint that she doesn't need to stay. I'm still freaked, but I think I'll be able to ask an intelligent question by the time I get to speak to someone.

One problem. I can't make myself walk through the door.

Being a nurse, Cheryl has surely seen it before. She pulls into an adjacent parking slot. Hops out of the car. Walks around to face me.

"How long has it been?" she asks. We both know the rest is, "since you were last in a hospital."

"Four and a half years."

She takes my hand, tugs lightly. Leads me through the door.

"I'll be alright," I claim.

"Of course, you will," she remarks. "Just like riding a bike."

I laugh. Not a big laugh, but it unlocks my muscles.

Cheryl precedes me to the reception desk, where she tells the woman behind the glass we're here for their new shooting patient.

"Name?"

"Bernie Beck," I volunteer from behind.

We are directed to the second-floor operating suite, and Cheryl is greeted warmly at the nurses' station. The woman who appears to be in charge tells us my dad is still in surgery.

"How badly has he been shot?" I ask.

"It's his leg," the nurse replies. "That's all I know right now."

My companion selects a chair in the waiting area and picks up a magazine.

I go over to assure her I'm okay, that she really can go home.

The woman's nurturing-nurse eyes say, "Bullshit." Aloud, she reminds me I don't have a car.

I concede defeat with a smile, and confess that I really appreciate the company.

Pointing her chin toward the officer pacing nearby, Cheryl suggests that he might like to speak with me.

"Now you're throwing a dog a bone?" I tease, because exchanging information with a cop is exactly what I want right now.

Cheryl disguises a grin by pretending to read the magazine.

"Officer Cameron," he responds to my introduction. Then he gestures to a small room set aside for sensitive conversations. He closes the door, and we sit opposite each other across a small table.

"Any witnesses?" I inquire.

The officer waves his head. "Tan car. A shopkeeper thought maybe a Kia."

Cameron is the military-haircut, square-jawed variety of cop. The silent, don't-give-anything-away sort. Professional, in other words. He may not be precisely who I should be speaking with, but he will know exactly who to bring in.

I tell him it's unlikely the shooting was random.

He weaves his fingers together and places them carefully on the table. "Go on…"

Glad for a productive way to camouflage the stress of my father's surgery, I relate everything from the mugging at my father's front door up to today, throwing in my concerns for Ana along the way.

While Cameron rubs his chin and processes, I check my watch. Three forty-five p.m. Dad's bank will be closing right about now.

Excusing myself, I step out and around a corner to call Sarah Brown, aka Trixie, the young woman who risked her job trying to help us.

She sounds breathless when she picks up. "You just caught me, Ms. Beck. What can I do for you?"

I explain, and she agrees to stay a few extra minutes to look over Ana's bank accounts one more time.

"Please text me whatever you find, one way or the other," I urge.

Much to my relief, she agrees.

Behind me, a tired surgeon emerges from an automatic door and surveys the waiting room.

"Lauren Beck?" he inquires of the half dozen sullen family members waiting for news.

I raise my hand and meet the surgeon halfway.

Almost as eager for the doctor's information as I, Officer Cameron hovers a discreet distance to the side.

"Your father came through surgery very well, Ms. Beck. We'll be keeping him here a few days, of course."

"When can I see him?"

"About another hour. When he's out of Recovery. Please keep it brief, though. He's going to be fine, but he's lost a lot of blood."

Cheryl has gravitated toward us, and the surgeon recognizes her. "Do you know this young lady?" he asks after they exchange greetings.

"Yes, Phil. Lauren was with me when she heard the news."

While they talk shop, I return to Officer Cameron. "My father was driving my car," I remark. "You happen to know where it is?"

"Strip mall on Gaberdine," he replies. Taking a hand out of his pocket, he dangles the keys between us. "All locked up."

"Thanks. My duffel's in there."

"And your Glock."

The police searched the Jeep. Of course, they searched my Jeep. Doesn't everybody?

"Old service piece?"

I nod.

"We know you were four miles away sipping tea."

"Cheryl vouched for me."

"While you were on the phone. I would take you to your car, but…" He hands me the keys.

"…but you have to stay here. Will you be guarding my dad tonight?"

"That'll be somebody else. But I'll probably still be here when you get back."

I slide into the chair next to Cheryl.

"Time to clock out, Nurse Anderson. Is the strip mall on Gaberdine on your way home?" Most likely Dad didn't drive far from her house to get our lunch.

"Yes, ma'am. That where your car is?"

"Yep."

While we're alone in the elevator, Cheryl uses the privacy to report something the surgeon shared with her. Namely, that the angle of my father's wound suggested he was leaning into the back of the Jeep when he was shot. "Lucky," she adds, because whatever he was reaching for saved him from a much more serious upper body shot.

When we arrive at the strip mall, she stops behind the Jeep to let me out.

I thank her a thousand times.

Then I tell her I'm very sorry about her daughter.

"I know you are," she says, "and I'm sorry about your father."

The rest gets said with a clasp of hands. Then I blow her a kiss, climb out of her little Ford, and shut the door. As I wave goodbye, I shout, "Don't' forget about the cat."

After she's gone, I take a moment to stand still. Soon the cars rushing on the road behind me become background noise. The woman ushering her son and daughter between cars toward the pizza restaurant disappear. A plane overhead quietly leaves its contrail, and a late afternoon breeze blows a wrapper across the parking lot.

I feel perfectly and blissfully alone. Just what I need to process this terrifying day.

With the Jeep angled into a slot facing the road, I see that the shooter must have passed between the two rows of parking spaces serving the five small businesses. Vehicles enter from the right, exit at a traffic light to the left. In other words, it's one-way past the back of the Jeep, making it possible the shooter was also the driver. The back of the Jeep opens like a door hinged on the left, so if Dad was leaning far enough in, his legs would have been the easiest target. Perhaps the only target.

Stop for a second. Pop. Floor it.

Since Dad was wearing jeans, I suppose it's possible he could have been mistaken for me. Unlikely, but possible. He might also have been the shooter's second choice, a warning to me to back off my search for Ana.

Dry, brown rivulets on the asphalt indicate that someone tried to rinse the spot where my father fell. Stepping over the sad evidence, I open the back of the Jeep and find a bag of sandwiches and a mess. The clothes in my duffel are ruffled, but the Glock is still here.

The heck with the filth and the diluted blood. I lie down on the macadam and scooch myself under the car. Look around as best I can, then feel around where I can't see.

After about three minutes of awkward fingertip searching, I locate the tracking device. Leaving it in place is probably a dangerous, backward way of getting information about Ana's whereabouts.

It may also be the only way.

Chapter 24

DAD LOOKS A BIT yellow around the gills when I take his free hand and settle onto the chair close to his bed. This is the first we've been alone since the surgeon removed the bullet from his leg.

"Hey," he says softly. "Cops don't cry."

"Daughters do," I whisper over the lump in my throat.

Dad squeezes my right hand. I grab two tissues from the little blue box on his tray table with my left.

There are tubes and monitors and a TV remote—all the trappings of a hospital room. Plus Officer Cameron is sitting outside the door, either flirting with nurses or guarding my father until he gets replaced. Whatever the case, I'm glad he's here.

Back down in Recovery, I allowed Cameron to speak with my father first. As the doctor ordered, the conversation was short.

Cameron: "Get a look at him?"

Dad: "Nope. Facing the wrong way."

Cameron: "Were you reaching for your daughter's gun?"

Dad: "Nope. Something else."

Cameron, holding up a tiny object: "This?" He showed Dad a tiny tube of wrinkle cream.

My father almost stopped breathing.

I relieve the officer of the embarrassing evidence. "Thanks," I exclaim. "I wondered what happened to that."

Dad did a pretty good job of hiding his relief.

At the moment, it seems he has nodded off. I'm just happy he's patched up, he's breathing, and he's holding my hand.

"You're doin' good, Dad," I whisper, trying not to awaken him. Yet, at least on some level, I'd like him to know I'm here.

"You'll be on crutches for a while," I add. *Several weeks actually.* "But they expect you'll regain your normal range of motion," *if he's lucky.* I know better than to torture either of us with something that hasn't happened yet.

"Anyway, whaddya know? I just found a tracker on the Jeep, which explains why I didn't pick up on a tail."

As if he's hoping for a whiff of whatever's for dinner, Dad draws in a deep breath.

I persist. "Who put it in place is the million-dollar question. Maybe Julian. But maybe not.

"Then there's Ana. If she's a captive, who's holding her? If she's free, is she with Julian? I just don't know, Dad. Anyway, I left the tracker where it is.

"Oh, and I phoned Sarah Brown at the bank again. She hasn't gotten back to me, but I caught her right at closing time. She's probably just being super careful." *Or she's blown me off.* Also possible.

"Listen, Dad. I missed lunch, and I'm starved. I'm gonna let you sleep for a bit, but I'll come right back. Okay?"

"Okay," he says, opening his eyes and adding a wink.

"You heard?"

"You're starving blah blah blah. Be right back…blah, blah. The cheesecake's supposed to be great here."

"Thanks for the tip. Don't go anywhere."

"Ha."

I ask Cameron if he wants anything from the cafeteria.

He replies that he's off duty as soon as he checks in with Dad one more time. We exchange cell numbers. Nod goodbye.

After sizeable portions of salad, Manhattan clam chowder, and macaroni and cheese, I am tucking into a slice of as-advertised cheesecake, when my phone dings.

I drop my fork and grab the instrument from the pouch on the side of my purse. It's dark outdoors now, super late for a bank employee to be texting about Ana's accounts. No matter. I'm thrilled to be getting any information anytime, anywhere.

The text is from Jack, the annoyingly good-looking Chief of Police back in New Mexico. It says, "Ana Beck using credit card. Call me."

I nearly choke on my cheesecake. This is great news. Monumental news...unless Ana's killer used the card—quick, before anyone finds out she's dead. Or unless the card was stolen, sold, or cloned.

I punch Jack's contact number with sticky fingers.

"Where is she? Do we know she used it personally? Talk, Jack. Tell me something good."

"Don't know about good, but it was used at a restaurant by a woman roughly matching Ana's description."

"How do you know what Ana looks like?"

"You showed me her picture."

"Oh, that. But how did the restaurant know what she looks like?"

"Lauren, slow down. Your stepmother is online like everybody else. She even has a website with a picture of herself and her artwork. Why are we talking about this?"

"Just making sure it's her, Jack. My father got shot. I think whoever's been trying to kill me put a tracker on the Jeep."

"What! When?"

"Today. Drive-by in the parking lot outside where he bought lunch."

Jack releases a huge breath. "And how the hell would I know any of that? Were you even going to tell me?"

"Jeez, Jack. I've been a little busy."

The girl in a candy-striped uniform who's been clearing up trash stands still as a pillar staring at me. I wiggle my fingers hello and turn away.

The girl steps a little closer. "You done with that?" she asks, and I realize she's not just eavesdropping, she's trying to finish her job and go home.

"Hold on, Jack."

I stab a white plastic fork into the last of my cheesecake, and push the tray aside. The cheesecake goes with me.

The girl collects the tray, and makes her escape.

The hallway is mercifully deserted, so I put my purse on the floor and, for sanitary purposes, sit the paper plate on top.

In as discreet a voice as I can manage, I describe the events of the last couple of days.

Jack and I agree that whether or not Ana left my father is mostly of interest to my father, and that, "Somebody really needs to make sure she's safe."

We also agree that person is me.

"So exactly where is this Mountain View Café?"

Jack gives me an address on Main Street, Braxton, Utah, a town about three and a half hours northwest of where I am, which is slightly south of Salt Lake City.

"If Ana uses the credit card again, you'll let me know?"

"Right away. But Lauren, please watch your back. This stalker/attacker, whoever he is, may not be a professional, but it doesn't take a genius to pull a trigger."

As if I hadn't thought of that.

Chapter 25

JULIAN COULD FEEL a panic coming on. His muscles twitched. His hands were sweaty. Before destroying his latest stolen credit card, he'd used it to buy food and fuel. Now he was running low again— on everything. He was hours away from his supplier, too.

The middle-of-nowhere camping facility was experiencing a turnover, so he wandered away from the activity. Eased himself down onto the edge of a damp RV pad. Braced his free hand behind him on the cement. And wondered how the hell to fix his life.

He'd slipped the campground owner an extra twenty to let him park his van overnight, use the shower, take a proper shit. He would have to leave soon, probably head farther north, but right now worrying about money was crowding everything else out of his head.

He had to call her.

She picked up on the second ring.

"I need help, Ma," he said immediately after hello.

"I'm fine, and how are you, Julie?"

"I'm in real trouble, Ma. You gotta help me."

"Why can't you talk nice to me just once, Julian? How come you treat your mother so bad?"

"Are you not hearing me? I said I'm in real trouble."

Silence.

"Ma?"

"What have you done this time? Tell me that, and I'll consider."

"I…I can't, Ma. You've gotta trust me. It's just…I screwed up. Please. I got nobody else." Hearing himself plead made him hate his mother even more.

"How much? Another fifteen hundred?"

"Real money, Ma. Twenty thou." He knew he was pushing it, but he had to try.

"Let me think about this."

Silence.

Julian's knee began a nervous bounce.

"If I do this, not another dime ever," Ana finally answered. "Not one dime.

Julian switched the phone to his other ear.

"And another thing," Ana continued. "If I can get it, and that's a big IF, I hand it to you in person."

Julian could scarcely believe it. All his life living on nothing, and now that she's got hers, she's busting his balls?

He conceded because he had to. "…but you can get it, right? You can get that much?"

"I'm still thinking about it, Julian. I'll let you know."

"When?"

"Tomorrow. Maybe the next day. I'll call."

Tomorrow.

Maybe the next day.

He would tell the campsite owner he thought the twenty bought him a second night.

Just let him try to toss him out.

Chapter 26

BEFORE SHE GOES off shift, one of Dad's nurses fixes me up with a recliner and bedding, and once again, I gather what I need from my bag in the Jeep, smuggle the Glock inside for safekeeping, and prepare myself to sleep in yet another makeshift situation. I'm all for being low-maintenance, but lately I've gained a new appreciation for my own bed.

Dad's snore is especially resonant with oxygen prongs in his nose, and when I finally sleep, I'm a hibernating bear. It takes the fragrance of eggs and bacon to lift my eyelids. Even then it is with reluctance.

Since Dad isn't exactly marching around, I make use of the room's bathing amenities, and dress in the fresh clothes I brought from the car. Only the jeans remain the same.

I am thrilled to see my father sitting up and eating with two hands. He slurps black coffee just like I remember, and dabs his lips each time with a folded napkin.

"Jack Jenkins called last night," I report when I think Dad's coffee has kicked in. "Ana's credit card was used up in Braxton, Utah."

Dad halts his toast in mid-air. "Ana's okay?" His joy is so effervescent he almost levitates off the bed.

I screw up my face. "Probably?" I say to temper his excitement. "Jack checked with the restaurant. The woman who bought dinner with the card did look like Ana, more or less."

Dad slaps the bed with his non-intubated hand. "That's great news, Beanie. Wow! Whaddya know. You've got a lead. Here."

He offers me his actual toast.

"Braxton's hours away, Dad. Who's going to sit and stare at you like a doting daughter?"

"Bah. I'm fine. I'll be doing laps around the hall in no time."

A nurse has wandered in to check whatever. "Soon, maybe," she agrees. "But finish your breakfast. We got tests to run. Charts to fill out. Don't forget your menu, by the way."

"See, Beanie? Who needs a doting daughter when I've got her? What's your name, dear?"

The nurse is a stocky African-American with gray hair tucked under a wide black headband. Her lips are pressed into a stern, feminist reprimand.

"What? What did I say?"

I deflect. "…that you'd like me to drive four hours north of here and leave you alone?"

"Yes!" Dad slaps the bed with the wrong hand and yelps with regret.

I confess I'm infected with optimism, too, just not as potent as his. It's been several days. If Ana is free to eat dinner in Braxton, Utah, why hasn't she called home?

One of many questions to ask, if I can find her.

Chapter 27

JULIAN HAD NO IDEA Yellowstone National Park was so big. It took him more than an hour to pick the best place for his mother to hand over the money, then twenty-three precious phone minutes telling her how to get there.

He had chosen the main visitors' area for Old Faithful, outside the second of two large, peak-roofed buildings serving everybody waiting to see the geyser erupt. When the time came and hundreds of tourists packed the stands and crowded the fenceline, he would steer his mother to the remote spot he picked, back toward where he parked, and behind some big bushes. After collecting the twenty grand, a quick sprint to the van, and he'd be gone.

And here she was, hustling toward him through the oncoming stragglers in another one of her ugly, multi-colored dresses. Shielding her eyes from the sun, she rose on her toes and flapped her chubby hands when she caught sight of him. Already her makeup looked as if it was dissolving in the heat.

He expected a sweaty hug, but she tucked a curl behind his ear instead.

"You look good, Julie."

"Ma!" he complained, ducking away. "I'm not a girl."

Ana huffed. "Oh, alright, *Jules*!" she corrected herself, irritably stuffing her hands into her pockets and casting her eyes to the ground.

Suddenly, there was a loud roar, joined by the crowd's own eruption. When Ana turned to watch, her mouth dropped open like some dumb kid who'd never seen anything like it.

Julian didn't bother turning his head. He grasped his mother's elbow and turned her toward the long walkway back toward the car park. As the splashing roars and crowd noise rose and fell, he had to tug on his mother's arm to keep her on track.

When they arrived at the spot he wanted, nobody else was within fifty yards. A newly arrived bus would be unloading any minute, but with luck they'd be finished before that.

"Do you have it?"

Ana wrapped her arms across her body as if preparing for a lecture. "Getting $20,000 in cash isn't easy, you know. Western Union caps the amount you can send…"

Impatience was sparking his anger. "Yeah, but do you have it?"

Ana peered at him so hard her eyes were nearly shut. "Is that all I get for my money? A grab and run like a thief?"

Julian's back stiffened, and his chin lifted. His cheeks tightened into a frown. His elbows squeezed against his waist while his fists thrust forward. His nose flared, and his breathing quickened.

Ana's brow creased with dismay. "I drove nine hundred miles for this?"

The bus passengers were still crowded together in the parking lot, but they would soon be passing by.

"Do…you…have…it?"

"No, Julian. I do not."

Julian staggered backward. What the hell was wrong with her? Had she really come this far just to screw him over?

An especially loud cheer started the children from the bus running to see what they were missing. Parents with no choice hustled to catch up.

Julian hissed into his mother's face. "Did you bring any money?"

"No, Julian. I did not. I couldn't. Western Union…"

Julian flung his arms over his head. Spun around until he faced his mother again.

"You bitch," he snarled, fists trembling with rage. "Why are you doing this to me?"

Dancing from foot to foot, he showed her the flat of his hand. "Gimme what you got."

Ana didn't move nearly fast enough, so he grabbed the purse off her arm. Rummaged inside for her wallet. Withdrew every bill it contained.

Then he looked at his mother with an intensity she hadn't seen before. "I'm in trouble, Ma. Big trouble. You gotta get the twenty grand. Two days, max. I'll call and tell you where I am, so don't go very far. Just get the money and call me," he begged. "I need this, Ma. Please don't let me down."

Ana stared at him openmouthed.

For a moment, he stared back.

Then he slammed her useless purse to the ground and ran.

Chapter 28

ANA WATCHED HER son run past the busload of
tourists and disappear among the parked cars. She was too
wired to cry, although a good cry was in her near future.

She knew why she'd angered him. She was angry
herself.

He seemed so indifferent, so callous…so frightened
that it frightened her.

Where had he been? That was all she'd wanted to
know. *What had he been doing?*

Well, now she knew: Nothing good.

With a herd of tourists streaming by like smiling
sheep, Ana began to walk.

She'd been living with her son treating her like
garbage for a while. The rudeness, the selfishness. She
had no idea why Julian had suddenly begun to despise
her, but she'd had plenty of exposure to such treatment.
When she was young, it seemed most of the men in her
village behaved like that. But just as the village women
chose to stay, Julian's callous attitude didn't keep her
from loving him.

Today felt different. Now that she was aware of how
desperately he needed money, she understood that if she
failed him, the last thin thread connecting them would
break. She also suspected giving in to him might produce
the identical result.

Back at her SUV, she wiped away sweat and sniffle
with a tissue from her purse, wrenched open the hot-to-
touch door handle. Leaving the door open for air, she sat
behind the wheel and turned her attention to her own
predicament. She'd been staying in cheap motels because

Julian told her not to use her credit card, but now that he'd taken all her cash, how was she to buy dinner? Home was more than nine hours away. Where was she supposed to sleep?

Still brooding about what to do about her ungrateful son, Ana began driving south.

Julian's first text arrived during the first hour. "So, are you getting it or what? I need to know."

With no answer to give him, she didn't bother to reply.

An hour later, her phone dinged while she was stopped for gas. "Answer me, Ma. Please. It's important."

The "please" gave Ana pause, but what was she to do? Give him hope, only to disappoint him if she decided not to comply?

She climbed back into the SUV and rejoined the speeding traffic.

Julian phoned almost immediately, but driving at seventy miles an hour was no time to conduct a weighty conversation.

She severed the call.

Fifty minutes later, she listened to Julian's voicemail at a stop light. "I need the twenty grand bad, Ma. Call me."

She would. When she was ready.

Ana chose the small town of Braxton, Utah, to stay the night, and was eating her dinner at the restaurant when Julian texted again. It said, "If you love me, you'll get it."

To help her swallow, Ana needed a sip of water. She was still uncomfortable with it all—the size of the request, the desperation in Julian's voice. Did she dare deny him? Was giving in really in her son's best interest?

She deleted the message.

Before going to sleep, she placed her cell phone on the night table by her head, so Julian's midnight call frightened her awake.

"It's life and death now, Ma. No joke. I'm a dead man if you don't come through."

Ana threw her legs over the edge of the bed. "What if I can't get it, Julian? What then?"

"You can, though. Can't you? Take a loan or something. It's my life we're talking about here."

And then Julian began to cry.

There would be no more sleep that night.

In the morning she set about getting $20,000 wired to a bank in the tiny mountain town where she'd landed. When she'd finished proving her identity to the bank manager, she walked down the street to the homey little café and ordered herself a tuna sandwich.

As she watched the few locals coming and going, her phone began to vibrate on the hard surface of the table.

"Do you have it?"

"Tomorrow, Julian," she answered.

"Good. Good! That's Tuesday, right? See you tomorrow night."

Ana described how to find her motel.

Chapter 29

FOR THE FIRST FEW hours driving northwest toward Utah, I am acutely aware of the surrounding traffic. I vary my speed in case of tagalongs, watch to see if any vehicles defy coincidence and seem dangerously familiar. Only when I'm past what I judge to be the tracking gadget's range will I dare focus on what curdles my innards the most: Ana has been gone nearly nine days, and I'm not even close to Braxton, Utah, the town where she recently charged meals.

Grateful for the soothing voice of the GPS that's keeping me on course, I've just passed by the Ute Mountain Reservation. The scenery around me feels vast—high skies and rocky, red-hued terrain dotted with low clumps of brush and sturdy-looking trees. The cool air mussing my hair smells spicy and warm. It's a shame I'm too worried to enjoy it.

Many miles later I stop for fuel and a stretch in Cortez, a modest, welcoming town toward the corner of Colorado. Just stepping out of the Jeep, I'm reminded that ordinary life still exists. I buy coffee and a sandwich and wish I could stay longer.

By 6 p.m. I'm in Utah and way too tired to continue. I'll need my wits about me when I get to Braxton, and there is little civilization on this section of my route.

When a three-story chain hotel magically appears up ahead, I slap the steering wheel with a happy "Yes," and pull in. When I get out, I take care not to nick the *Harold's Fun-for-All Circus* advertised in silver and gold script on the truck next to me, one of three in the lot.

To the right lies a squat box of a building with a disproportionately large sign proclaiming "George's Family Restaurant." Butt-sore from driving all day, walking into a casual eatery with real wooden tables and plastic placemats makes me sigh with relief. The fragrance of beef gravy and buttered noodles from the tray passing by makes my stomach rumble.

A harried waitress tells me to sit anywhere, so I wend my own way down the aisle to a four-seater against the wall beside five bandy guys I imagine to be circus employees. They're drinking tall, frothy beers, perhaps enjoying an overnight break between shows. I can't catch their conversation, but I enjoy the dramatic gestures of a nearly toothless fellow with arms ropy enough to wrestle an octopus.

Another waitress in pink and white hands me a paper menu. To help me relax, I order a white wine and the turkey-dinner special, which includes stuffing and cranberries. No pumpkin pie, but bread pudding with caramel sauce.

I am half asleep from alcohol and turkey tryptophan when I finally check in at the hotel. While the clerk runs my card, I pick up a Harold's Fun-for-All Circus flier from the counter. The descriptions of frolicking clowns, astounding acrobats, "the breathtaking Borman high-wire act," and "our special sideshow starring Harold the Hypnotist" sweep me back to a night out with my father soon after my mother died. Not bothered by clowns, I freaked over a much more realistic danger—the tiger.

With room key and duffel in hand, I am headed for the hotel elevator when my phone dings. It's a text from the bank employee I call Trixie.

"A. Beck wired $20,000 to bank in Braxton, Utah, on Monday. Cashed out 2 p.m. today."

I text back an understated, "Thanks," and embellish it with a thumbs-up emoji.

Almost certainly, Julian has collected the money from his mother by now.

If he is working alone and has no intention of harming her, fine.

But if the young criminal-in-training is involved with anyone more dangerous than he, Ana Tomas Beck probably just became expendable.

And that, "Ladies, gentlemen, and kids of all ages," frightens me more than a dozen tigers.

Chapter 30

IDEALLY NEAR THE state highway, the gas station was also free from the bright lights of civilization. Parked among the few vehicles waiting for service, his latest stolen car looked quite at home.

He wore dark clothes and leather gloves. A baseball cap shadowed his pale skin. Taut with adrenaline, he paced the tarmac, punching his palm with impatience.

"Damn! Where is that kid?" Julian was supposed to arrive two hours after closing.

"Just one more payoff," he'd drilled into the kid, "and our worries are over."

He leaned against a nearby car bumper and wished he could smoke.

When the white van arrived ten minutes later, he bolted upright and slapped the driver's door before the vehicle rolled to a stop.

"A few more feet," he ordered as soon as Julian lowered the window a crack.

"You got it." The vehicle inched forward its own length and stopped.

The garage's security spotlights illuminated the rear doors perfectly now. But when they were yanked open, the hinges screeched loud enough to scare a flock of sleeping birds out of the trees.

Curious what was going on, Julian twisted around and caught him arm-deep in his duffle bag.

"Hey! Leave my stuff alone." The kid jumped out and hustled around to confront him.

He stopped himself just in time. "Com'on, man. What're ya doin'?"

"Protecting myself."

Julian spread his arms in protest. "From me? I never threatened to kill *you*. You had me scared shitless."

"Yes, and she fell for it, didn't she? Now quit bitchin' and get back in the van. I'll be done in a minute."

When they were both seated and ready to go, Julian attempted to clear the air. "What were you looking for anyhow? A weapon?"

No answer meant yes, so the kid extracted a jackknife from his jacket and snapped the blade open. "Like this?"

The man snickered. "Put that away, kid."

Julian made a show of closing the blade against his leg and slipping the harmless handle back into his pocket.

"Drive," the older man ordered. "Let's get this thing done."

***

Twice Ana had considered changing her motel room. The hum of the beverage machines in the passthrough immediately to the right could be heard through the wall, and twice the sound of ice dropping into the machine's metal bin woke her up. Too late to bother now, though. She'd be leaving first thing in the morning.

She smiled into the mirror as she touched up her makeup. She had already showered and put on a loose, flowered dress. With her figure, the close-fitting jeans and leggings other women wore just emphasized her extra weight. She'd be meeting Julian inside her room anyhow, so warmth wasn't an issue.

It would go better this time. Surely $20,000 put her in charge. Julian wouldn't dare deny her a couple simple answers with that much at stake.

She had just zipped up her makeup case when he tapped on her door.

"Open up, Ma."

Mustn't appear too eager, Ana counseled herself, as she sauntered over to let her son in. Intending to draw him into a hug, she swung the door wide.

She got one glimpse of Julian's face before a dark figure grabbed her shoulders and spun her around. A gloved hand covered her mouth. Long legs pushed hers farther into the room.

"Lock the door," the stranger barked.

Julian hastened to obey.

"Gag!"

A rolled bandana was thrust roughly between her lips and tied tightly behind her head.

The stranger shoved her onto the edge of the bed.

When she began to roll away, he slapped her.

She shot Julian a desperate glance, but he didn't notice.

"Blindfold!"

Julian nodded.

As her son tied a black rag around her head, Ana recognized the horrifying truth. Julian was helping this man get her money, and after tonight…

A needle pricked her arm through the sleeve of her dress.

***

"What'd you give her?" Julian asked.

"Just a little G," the older man answered. "Make our job easier."

"Liquid X! You can inject that? I thought you had to…"

"Put it in a drink? Uh, no. Not my style."

"You're not going to…?"

"Rape her? Not why we're here."

Ana's body was already limp, her cheeks shiny with sweat.

"Shit," the man swore. "G doesn't usually…" Disgusted, he shoved the woman further back on the bed.

Julian's mind had trouble keeping up. He'd expected to enter the motel room alone, then tell Ma they had to hurry. She would hand over a big envelope of cash. He'd duck back outside. They would quickly split the money, celebrate with a fist bump, and get the hell outta there. Julian in his van, the older man in his mother's blue SUV, which would shortly be abandoned.

Finished.

Done.

Over.

"Look for it!"

The order snapped Julian back to the present.

His mother's purse was over on the chair. Hurrying toward it, he rounded the bed so quickly he tripped on the corner of the bedspread. Annoyed, he unzipped the soft leather sack and dumped its contents on the chair. Sunglasses, lipstick, tissues, keys, and a thin red wallet lay in a messy pile. Nothing remotely resembled an envelope thick enough to contain $20,000. Julian pocketed what cash there was while the other man tugged rings off his mother's pudgy fingers.

While he was raking through the few clothes his mother hung in the closet, his partner found the large brown envelope in the righthand night table. Stretched to the seam with cash, it was immediately tucked behind the old man's belt and hidden by his shirt and jacket.

"So, what now? We split it and go?"

"Not so fast, kid. We've got to finish…" He gestured toward the unconscious body draped across the bed.

"Why can't we just leave?"

"What do you think will happen when the maid comes in tomorrow, eh? The cops'll be all over this."

"So…?"

"So, when we're sure everybody's asleep, we take her into the woods and…"

"…and what? Kill her? Can't we just, you know…tie her to a chair or something?"

"You hate her. What do you care?"

"Yeah, but…"

Even after the neighboring lights had been out for two hours and they'd begun to haul Ana's comatose body into the woods, Julian still didn't know what would happen when they got there.

Chapter 31

AFTER A SLEEP PUNCTUATED with nightmare awakenings and a breakfast buffet I could scarcely taste, I drove with hands clenched on the Jeep's wheel and eyes darting as if I were still being pursued. I arrived at Main Street, Braxton, Utah, about 10 a.m.

Turns out Braxton is tiny, the sort of town so small and spare you wonder how anyone makes a living here. It is also beautiful, if you like winding roads and rocky hills studded with pines and aspen.

As of last night, no room has been charged on Dad and Ana's joint credit card, so it's reasonable to assume she is still here somewhere. With that in mind, I park near the center of town in front of a Walgreens and use a phone app to search for places where Ana may be staying. Hotels and B&Bs there are none, and no one at any of the six motels admits to a visitor of Ana's name or description. I suppose I could check each motel's parking lot for a blue SUV, but with everything so far apart, probably a last resort.

Squeezing the phone as if wringing its expensive little neck, I step out onto the sidewalk.

I pace.

Then I phone the nearest hospital.

No patients by the name of Ana Tomas Beck.

I pocket the phone, grab my purse, lock the Jeep, and set off on foot toward the bank where Ana picked up $20,000 in cash.

Beside the door to the bank's narrow storefront is a pot of purple and white petunias. In its shade sits a bowl of water meant for passing dogs. I suspect the dogs are also invited inside and will receive biscuits if they behave themselves. It's that sort of town.

There is one teller, and one manager manning a partitioned-off desk.

I place my hands expectantly on the back of the manager's visitor chair.

Wearing khakis and a short-sleeved, dark green polo shirt sporting the bank's pine tree insignia, he rises to shake my hand. Waves me onto the chair with a smile.

"What can I do for you, young lady? Open a checking account?" He knows I'm a stranger, as surely as everyone else in town will know.

"Not today," I say to let him down lightly.

"How then?"

With his long, bony fingers woven together on the desk, he listens with growing anxiety as I explain how a thirty-year-old ex Pennsylvania cop happens to be in Braxton, Utah, on a sunny Wednesday in September.

When I get to the part about Ana's unusual transaction, his thin face ages and pales. What were endearing smile-creases a moment ago are now gouges down the sides of his cheeks.

"No. No one was with her," he answers with remembered distress. "And no, Ms. Beck did not appear excessively stressed."

"Twenty thousand dollars," I muse. "What would that look like...roughly?"

"In twenties? It barely fit into an eight and a half by eleven envelope. Is that what you mean?"

"Yes, thank you.

"You were worried about her," I remark. We both know that almost no legal transactions involve large amounts of actual cash anymore.

"I was, very much so. I walked her to her car personally, just to be sure she was safe. She isn't, is she? Safe, I mean."

"I'm not sure," I answer honestly. "That's what I'm trying to find out."

When I shake his hand goodbye, I swear it's stone cold.

Next, the Mountain View Café, the lovely spot down the block where Ana ate the evening she arrived. Also, three times the next day, and twice the following.

At the moment, it's slightly late for lunch, so showing Ana's wedding picture doesn't inconvenience the staff too terribly much. One waitress lounges over the counter from the inside to consider Ana's face. The other leans against one of the stools, while the lone cook eavesdrops from his side of the passthrough. The whole place probably seats thirty people, if twenty of them are good friends. Five are now lingering over…hard to say what. I guess they're just lingering.

"Yeah, yeah," the first waitress pipes up after a moment's consideration. "We know her. Out-of-towner. Hard to miss."

"Pretty hair," was the other's observation. "Sweet face."

The first girl held the picture at the passthrough for the cook to see.

"Oh, yeah," he concurs. "Ordered the chicken pot pie twice."

"Only time that's happened," the inside waitress jokes.

"Get stuffed, Janine," he calls back, his eyes never lifting from his spatula.

"The credit card charges go through for last night yet?" I inquire. Ak crucial question, which I try not to show.

The girls glance at each other. "Do bears shit...," the older begins, but the cook intervenes.

"Hey, don't talk like that in front of the lady."

"Oh? And what, pray tell, do you think 'Get stuffed,' means Tommy boy?"

"It means 'Get stuffed, Janine. Now leave me the hell alone. I got food to cook."

Janine takes pity on me. "The owner is anal about getting paid. No grass grows on his ass, if you know what I mean."

It's now mid-afternoon, and I'm resting on a rustic bench facing a tall chainsaw carving of woodland animals perfectly centered at the intersection of Main Street and Aspen Avenue. I confess I'm sweating in the long-sleeved T-shirt I grabbed this morning in honor of the altitude.

I am also frustrated enough to carve a tree trunk with my teeth.

I lift off my baseball cap and wipe my brow with my sleeve. A car drives by, and I'm grateful for the breeze. When it's gone, I fan myself, slug down some of the cold water I bought in Walgreens, and try to think.

Human nature probably explains why the desk clerks I spoke to this morning refused to say whether Ana was there. Five times out of six they were probably telling the truth. Regarding the sixth, he or she was either lazy, ornery, or excessively cautious. The latter person would have become suspicious just because I asked. Having to ask meant Ana wasn't expecting me, so he or she took the high road and protected their paying customer's privacy.

So now I'm sitting here in the sun like a deadbeat with nothing to do because I'm actually not sure what's left. Everything I'm learning—and not learning—contributes to my anxiety. It feels like I'm confined in a rubber suit that's shrinking by the minute.

Dad picks up after two rings on the direct line to his hospital room.

"Hey, Dad," I say, taking a stab at sounding cheerful.

"Hey to you, too, Beanie. What's up?" He doesn't bother trying to sound happy. He sounds as if he's been holding his breath waiting for me to call.

"I'm in Braxton, Utah. Sitting on a bench smack in the middle of it actually."

Dad breathes.

"You haven't found her yet."

"Nope." I report what I've done so far.

"You talk to the police?"

"They seem to be in short supply. I'm guessing Utah's state troopers cover areas the size of Texas."

"That remote?"

"Yup."

"Oh, well. My bet's on you anyhow."

I know that. Hence, the shrinking rubber suit.

"Check your credit card today?"

He has not.

I wait.

"Nothing since lunch yesterday." He mentions the Mountain View Café where I'd just had chicken pot pie for lunch. I also dawdled over some chocolate ice cream hoping my missing stepmother might wander in.

She did not.

I ask Dad about his leg.

He tells me he's coming along nicely. "Might even get released soon."

I stifle a gasp. I've been so focused on Ana I didn't consider where Dad might go if he gets discharged.

"No worries," he says, as if he read my mind. "Your friend Cheryl offered to pick me up if you can't. She said I can stay in her spare room until you can get back down." Cheryl, the grieving mother and nurse who drove me to the hospital, then supported me through the worst of my fears.

"Wow," is all I can manage. "That's…that's…"

"It's a good deal, Beanie. Admit it."

"Waitaminute. Cheryl told you in person? You've seen her again?"

"She dropped in." Once a nurse, always a nurse.

"I've only been gone overnight."

"Feels longer."

I had to agree. Curiously, the minutes away from Dad feel like months. It's only when I'm intent on finding Ana they feel like seconds.

I really, *really* need to get back to that.

We ring off with fond farewells, but what troubles me anew is what my dad didn't say. Ana charged consecutive meals for three days in a row. But, as the waitresses confirmed, nothing last evening. If she's still here, where did she have dinner?

Returning to the Mountain View Café, I ask if there are any other places Ana might have eaten, and the waitress named Janine mentions a barber/hairdresser who sells sandwiches to her customers. "They're usually gone by one, though."

"Grocery store?"

"Sure. A little far away. But sure."

At this point, I'm not sure about anything.

Janine seems to be waiting for me to say something else, possibly because I haven't moved.

So, I ask the ridiculous thing that's been bothering me. Not urgently. More like a dusty table that begs to be wiped every time you walk by.

"Have there been any child abductions around here lately?"

Janine draws in a breath, twists her apron in her hand. "No, not here. Up in Thomasville last year." She shakes her head. "My sister's neighbor's kid. I've got a daughter...."

"Is Thomasville nearby?"

"Twenty minutes or so. Are you thinking that's what happened? Because Tammy was only twelve, and..."

...and Ana is considerably older.

"Yeah, yeah. You're right." I recant. "Just a wild thought."

A wild, nagging thought, probably brought on by that billboard. Like when you finally buy a new car, you notice other cars for a couple weeks.

I thank the helpful waitress once again. Step outside. Return to my bench.

Motel staffs usually change shifts about now, so maybe I'll get lucky if I simply start over. Use my charm. Or prevaricate.

Or both.

Beats driving for hours checking parking lots for Ana's SUV.

"She's a missing person of interest to the Albuquerque police," I try on the first call.

No go.

I sigh into the desk-man's ear. "...*because* she left home without her meds." My new stepmother is too young to have any regular meds, so I'm probably telling the truth.

Dial tone.

The third motel clerk hesitates just long enough to stiffen my spine.

"She's there, isn't she?" I press.

"Not anymore," he replies. "You planning on paying her bill, because she skipped that little detail..."

"You bet," I tell him. "I'll be right there."

Chapter 32

THE WHISPERING PINES MOTEL is snuggled up against a forest of tall pointy evergreens and some deciduous trees I can't name. It has egress in three directions—left and right onto the two-lane road out of Braxton, plus another exit onto a side road aiming east. I think the office and two angled rows of rooms are meant to simulate log cabins, except there are no logs involved, just horizontal planks of wood painted dark brown punctuated with white window frames in need of a touch-up.

I park near the office on the left of the short macadam lot and hustle in. It is only in passing that I realize there is no blue Chevy SUV bearing a New Mexico license plate parked outside.

A young man wearing a smirk and a light blue denim shirt is leaning on his desk waiting for me. He doesn't appear to have much else to do.

"I called," I remark unnecessarily.

"So you did," he concurs.

"She hasn't come back," I remark, also unnecessarily.

"Not in the last fifteen minutes. You get lost or what?"

I pull a strand of hair off my sweaty cheek and give the whole handful a twist so it stays off. I do not need another irritation right now.

"I'm really not in the mood for jokes," I warn. "My stepmother's been missing for nine days, and this is the only place I know for sure she's been."

The desk clerk waves his head and clicks his cheek. "Wow. That's too bad. She skip out on her landlord, too?"

I try sighing, but my edginess remains. "Look, what's your name?"

"Luke."

"Listen, Luke. Can we please skip the cute crap and talk this out? I think the woman is in danger, and when I think that, I'm usually right."

"Well, good for you. You got some sorta spidey senses or something? Nobody likes…"

"I'm a private investigator," I interrupt. Private investigator in lower case letters, although I don't think this guy will care a fig about the difference.

"May I see her room?"

My nemesis folds his arms across his chest. "Where you staying tonight?"

It is already late afternoon, and I will need someplace to sleep.

I also need information, and this guy has it.

"Here," I answer. "Definitely here."

Clearly gloating, he says, "Whaddya wanna know?"

"I *wanna* see Ana's room."

"Waste of time."

"Why?"

"Room's empty. Her stuff is right here." He gestures toward a large green trash bag dumped against the wall next to a waste basket.

"Okay. May I see her stuff?"

"You gonna pay her bill?"

"You ran her credit card already, didn't you?"

"Sure, but Uncle Ralph insists on a checkout signature. More of a leg to stand on, if you know what I mean."

"Okay. Why don't I just sign the original bill?"

"Deal."

"Double or single for you?"

"Single is fine."

"Smoking?"

"Non-smoking, please."

Transaction complete, I receive an old-fashioned brass key to Room 5, next door to where Ana actually slept.

The owner's nephew hoists the bag of her belongings across the desk, and I lower it to the floor before I ask the obvious questions. "Did she have any visitors?" "Did you see her leave?"

"No." "No," and "I was off last night."

"Any other guests around?"

"You see any on your way in?"

Negative.

The non-answers feel like a full-stop, brick-wall defeat.

I roll my head to release some tension, then hoist the trash bag to my shoulder. I thank Nephew Luke and leave him to his crossword puzzle, or video game, or whatever he does when he's alone with his snarly thoughts.

I proceed along the row of rooms to the one just before Ana's. Inside, it smells of dust and dampness, as if it hasn't been used for a while.

Dumping my stepmother's belongings onto the one double bed, I go through the items one at a time.

Used clothing, mostly. Enough for a couple days, but certainly not nine. The toiletries you'd expect. Makeup, which makes sense. Dad says she doesn't leave home without it.

I flop down on the one existing chair, which faces the television. It is wooden, padded with worn green fabric, and equipped with small rollers for easy repositioning. There are a dresser, and two night tables flanking the one double bed. A bathroom is just around the corner from the TV. All in all, the space offers just enough walking room for two adults.

Restless, I wander over to the front window and spend a few moments gazing out at the parking lot. The afternoon light is just beginning to dim, partly from the forest behind, partly from some cloud cover moving in. It's a soft time of day, much kinder than noon's harsh sun. Looking forward to dinner and some rest, I draw the drapes. Step outside to collect my things from the Jeep.

A cleaning cart sits outside the open door to Room 6.

Trying not to startle the cleaner, I knock on the doorjamb and call out, "Hello?"

A pregnant girl giggles at herself as she rises from an uncomfortable crouch. It seems she's been picking up a candy wrapper.

"Ooh," she huffs. "You surprised me."

"Hi. I'm Lauren. I'm staying next door, and I'm told this was my stepmother's room. Are you done cleaning it?"

"Yeh, almost. You looking for something in particular?"

"I've been looking for her, but I guess I missed her."

"Too bad," the girl commiserates. She looks exhausted, and clearly needs to go home, so I quickly ask the same questions I asked the clerk.

Her answers are equally unhelpful.

My eyes scan the neatly made bed, the mirror layout to my room, the TV, bathroom and...no chair.

My hands and arms tingle. The knot in my chest feels as large as a boxing glove.

I wave to the pregnant girl and tell her, "Thanks."

Then I step back from the doorway and ease around the corner into the passthrough.

I don't know what the missing chair means, and have no clue why I feel such a buzz of anxiety, but I know better than to dismiss my fear.

Something happened here.

To the left, an ice bin and a beverage machine hum wearily. Behind me lies the parking lot. Straight ahead, the woods.

I take one tentative step toward the trees.

Two.

Three, only faster. I'm at the edge of the back-access's macadam in fifteen more strides.

When I spot two drag marks in the pine straw spaced like chair legs, I begin to run.

A hundred yards later I spot Ana.

She is wearing a flowered dress but no shoes. Her chin lolls against her chest, and she is tied to the chair.

She appears to be dead.

Chapter 33

WITH $20,000 TUCKED under his belt, the older man's urge to flee was nearly unbearable.

Moving the unconscious woman into the woods had been a risk, but one worth taking. Aside from a smoother getaway, it gave the kid time to process the inevitable.

Without question, the odds of manipulating Julian into doing it himself were steep. Still, it was worth a try. Pull it off and Julian didn't dare turn against him. Not ever. No matter what.

He started reasoning with the kid back in the motel room. Continued in hushed tones the whole time they were lugging Julian's mother uphill and out of sight.

"Well?" he pressed now. "What'll it be?"

Fifty-fifty, he figured. Heads, yes. Tails, no. Okay, either way.

Tails, he would deal with Julian the way he dealt with any other liability.

***

Depositing his mother on the rolling chair had gotten them across the back parking lot faster. Then the macadam ended and the woods began. Aside from dragging the extra chair weight uphill, the tree shadows made it impossible not to trip on rocks and tree roots and holes in the ground. When Julian wasn't struggling to stay upright, his arms and legs were being raked by the pine trees' dead lower branches.

Suddenly, the older man stopped, and just as suddenly Julian was sorry.

"Okay, kid. You know what comes next."

The break in the trees where they stood offered enough starlight for Julian to make out his mother's plump arms and flowered dress. Watching her chest lift and recede with a sleeper's sigh, he waved his head as if dismissing the past. All those, "Why can't yous," and, "You should haves." Over. Now she was just a clueless woman gagged and blindfolded by her own stupidity. What did she think was going to happen after she delivered that much cash? Julian might have spit with disgust if his mouth wasn't so dry.

"Well? What'll it be?"

By now Julian knew exactly what he was expected to condone.

He also knew how dangerous it would be to argue.

"Women always talk," had been tonight's sermon, and Julian recognized the truth in the words. How many times had he fled the room to avoid his mother's lectures? How many times had he wished she would just shut the hell up?

Julian couldn't see the man's stare, but he felt its force.

When car lights swept across the lower edge of the woods, they both froze.

The vehicle turned left across the back of the motel and stopped. One car door slammed. Then another.

Neither man was prepared to survive an escape through the woods. That, along with their unresolved argument, rooted them in place.

"I'll do it," Julian announced in the same low volume they'd been using. "You go."

The older man released his breath. "Good. Good! You're sure?"

The blade of Julian's jackknife snapped into place.

The older man turned and ran.

Chapter 34

FEARING THE WORST, I rush to Ana's side, touch her neck to feel for a pulse.

It's there, but faint. Her skin is chilly and lax, as if from dehydration.

"Ana! Can you hear me?"

A slight stirring makes my heart pound so hard I can almost hear it.

Her eyes blink open and slowly meet mine.

"I'm Lauren, Bernie's daughter," I tell her. "I'm going to get you some help."

Set in deep mascara shadows, the eyes that so mesmerized my dad close once again, perhaps with relief.

Stepping aside, I tap 9-1-1 into my phone. After identifying myself and reporting the nature of the emergency, I beg for an ambulance and the police. "We're about a hundred yards into the woods behind Whispering Pines Motel," I tell the dispatcher. "Hurry. Please, hurry."

"Yes, ma'am!" she concurs.

We disconnect, and I quickly switch to my phone's camera. I'll be altering a crime scene just as fast as I can get back from my room, but first a minute to shoot photographs for the authorities. Heavy clouds have moved in. A downpour could start any moment.

The camera lens captures enough evidence of Ana's horrific experience to make a hardened cop feel sick. Her flowered dress is caked with vomit, the air rank with excrement. Knowing she didn't charge dinner last night means she's been here since late yesterday afternoon, at least twenty-four hours.

A red bandana lies near the chair, and the way it's knotted suggests it was used as a gag. A small cut near Ana's right ear tells me whoever removed it nicked her in the process. Were it left in place, most likely she would have choked to death.

He, and I have a pretty good idea who *he* is, also allowed Ana to yell for help. Unfortunately, whoever called the shots made sure she was so far into the woods no one would hear her cries. A cold-blooded calculation by an experienced sociopath.

Slightly uphill, I notice a black rag with a strands of Ana's long dark hair stuck in a knot. Probably a blindfold, easily slipped off her head by whoever removed the gag. Lighter in weight than the bandana, at some point it must have blown several feet from where it was dropped.

Done taking photos, I touch Ana's arm. "I promise I'll be right back. I need something to cut those zip ties," the ones securing her to the chair.

I'm breathless from the downhill sprint when I arrive at my room. No sirens have pierced the relative silence—not yet anyway—a reminder that this is rural Utah.

There's a Swiss army knife on my keychain, and I toss that, a wet wash rag, a towel, and a bottle of water onto the motel's blanket. Gathering the corners, I sling the makeshift sack over my shoulder, slam the door behind me, turn into the passthrough, and break into a run.

Ducking branches and watching the uneven ground, I make my way back to Ana with thunder rumbling in the distance.

Circulation returning to Ana's swollen hands must hurt like hell, but she's too dazed and exhausted to make a sound. And yet she tracks my every move.

I wash her face, her lips. Offer her some water.

She thanks me with a nod.

"Don't move too much until the medics arrive. Okay?"

Another nod.

Carefully, I wrap the blanket around both her and the chair. When I've finished tucking in her bare feet, I'm facing her eye to eye.

Taking nothing for granted, I ask whether it's okay to call my father. "He's been worried sick about you."

Ana's face wilts. "Yes, please," she whispers.

I press the number of Dad's hospital room, and breathe with relief when he answers.

"I found her," I tell him over the lump in my throat. "Yes, she's alive."

When I check whether Ana wants to say hello, she nods eagerly, so I hold the phone against her ear to spare her aching hands.

"Bernie?"

Her voice sounds ancient, like someone's great-great-grandmother's ghost.

I'm close enough to hear Dad tell her it's the most beautiful sound he's ever heard.

***

Between the county hospital staff and the Utah Highway Patrol, aka state police, I am kept busy well into the night. Since the owner's nephew gave me everything from Ana's motel room when I paid her bill, I can supply the make, model, and license number of Ana's blue SUV. The authorities immediately place an APB on it, also on Julian's known white van. Yet after such a lengthy head start, locating either man by way of his vehicle seems pretty unlikely.

Now that anybody can buy a cheap police scanner on the Internet, I become the target of three separate reporters, each of whom pounce on my emergency call like bloodhounds on beef. To avoid having Ana's story spun as a dicey family drama, I tell them, "No comment," in turn, then hide out in the hospital's chapel until I'm sure all three have given up and gone home.

Meanwhile, the county hospital staff sets to restoring Ana to a semblance of her former self. Dehydration and hypothermia are apparently the top priorities. Assuming the many tests they administer don't reveal anything unexpected, she may be released in a day or so.

The police have been allowed a moment or two with the patient, but no more. Not tonight. They will get another chance late tomorrow morning, "if she's up to it." With potential visitors in mind, Ana asked me to bring her a certain sweater and some makeup.

So, yes. Physically she shows signs of recovery.

Emotionally? Different story, as is every traumatic experience.

It broke Ana's heart to admit her son accompanied the man who drugged her. Almost certainly, Julian helped drag her into the woods as well. Although she was unconscious when someone cut off the gag and removed the blindfold, it comforts Ana to think it was Julian. My opinion: Considering the sacrifices she made for him, the least he could have done.

It's midnight now, and I'm finally back at the motel. I've collected a clean blanket and plodded my way back to my room for a lengthy night's rest.

Tomorrow is another day, as usual.

It just won't be a usual day.

Chapter 35

I'M WELL AWARE there is no need to visit anyone in the hospital until after lunch. Been there. Tried that.

Instead, I spend the morning quizzing anyone who was around about the evening Ana was ambushed—stray guests, the pregnant cleaning girl, the motel night clerk by phone. Nobody saw or heard anything useful.

By the time I return to the hospital, Ana has had time for a lengthy nap and is absorbed in a TV soap opera. Without disturbing her, I detour to the central nurse's station. After explaining my relationship to her patient, Ana's nurse-of-the-day honors me with an update.

Physically, the report is better than I expected, mostly dehydration, hypothermia, bruises, sore wrists, and other, more minor, complaints.

Emotionally is probably a quite different story.

"Is she up to a talk with me?" I inquire hopefully.

The nurse, a soft-bodied, motherly sort, answers with a guarded yes. "Nothing too stressful," she cautions.

I tell her I'm just hoping to get better acquainted with my new stepmother. "We didn't meet under the best of circumstances."

She waves me down the hall with a warm smile. "I've got just the spot for you."

At the end of a row of patients' rooms is a beautiful solarium with cushioned furniture upholstered in a topical leaf pattern. The outer wall is all windows. A few small palm trees and potted ferns freshen the air, and a vase of red carnations decorates an end table. For a room that requires daily sanitizing, it's about as homey as you can get.

Just in case, I choose a seat next to an end table holding a box of tissues.

In a few minutes the motherly nurse wheels Ana in along with a rolling post with high hooks for holding Ana's hydration. The wheelchair? Maybe to conserve her strength.

We sit diagonally across from each other with cardboard cups of coffee from the corner niche. Ana begins with a generic question about my experiences so far as an adult.

"Your father told me about your health problem, but not much about what you've been doing since."

I appreciate being spared the story of Dad nursing me through Hodgkin's Disease, especially the part about my fiancé dropping me because I got sick. It's equally unlikely that Dad mentioned how I sequestered myself in my cancer counselor's attic apartment for four years, even after I got well.

"I became an insurance investigator there for a while," I hedge. "Then I bartended when I was staying with my brother and his wife on their farm. Is that what you mean?"

Looking amazingly fit for a person who went through hell, Ana's complexion and the drip bag are the most visible clues to her ordeal. Her dark hair falls inches beyond her shoulders in a beautiful cascade of waves. Her makeup is perfection. The hospital gown and cardigan are plain as can be, but on her they look surprisingly ladylike.

She folds her hands together on her lap, then looks me in the eye, "You miss being with the police, don't you?"

"How can you tell?"

Ana laughs. "It's obvious, isn't it?"

"I guess," I concede with a smile, "only it's not as simple as it seems. When I was on the job, I found a way to shake off the horrible things I saw. Not so much anymore. What happened to you…?" I shake my head.

"So, you tend bar to protect yourself?"

"Not exactly. I'm content with very little now. Happy even."

Ana plucks at the thin fabric covering her thigh. "I understand. More than you can probably know, I understand."

"You're happy with my dad, aren't you?"

"Yes. Very."

"He's happy with you, too. Happier than I've ever seen him."

"We're not talking about what we should, are we?" Ana remarks.

"No," I agree. "We are not."

She breathes deeply. Glances over my shoulder to the remote little town below, still damp from the overnight rain.

"Go ahead," she instructs, facing me front on. "Ask your police questions. I promise to tell you the truth."

Relieved not to be tiptoeing across broken glass, my body releases its tight grip on itself.

"I need to know more about your son. A lot more. I think you realize that."

Ana's eyes cast downward, but soon lift to meet mine. "What kinds of things?"

"Mostly what your relationship is really like."

"From the beginning?"

"Yes, please."

Visibly stiffening with resolve, Ana lifts her chin and stares me down. "Your father doesn't know this," a preface as binding as a contract.

Satisfied by my nod, she draws in a deep breath.

"I was raped when I was fifteen," she says. "Julian was born nine months later."

Questions clamor in my brain. "But…?" and "Why not…?" And yet I don't dare ask.

Observing my internal struggle, Ana fills in the blanks.

"Keeping the baby was meant to be my punishment. My father's exact words, 'Raising a child will teach you not to be so shameless.' Shameless." She huffs at the memory. "I wore lipstick. Like every other girl in my class, I wore lipstick."

She plucks at her lap again. Bravely lifts her head. "I knew of a clinic, but had no way to get there. Forty miles. It might as well have been on the moon."

She rustles on her chair and grows wistful.

"In the end, it didn't matter. The moment Julian was born he became everything to me. I worked seven grueling years in the fields until I could afford to come to the United States. I married a man dying of AIDS because he offered me and my son a permanent home. You can guess most of the rest."

She takes another moment to reflect before going on. "I thought Julian understood what fueled my decisions. Why I was always working. What he means to me.

"Turns out all he felt was deprived."

Her thoughts travel to the window scene and back.

"Very early on there was Monty, the stockbroker. Nice, type-A man. A little intense for my taste, but Julian followed him like a lovesick sheep. Unfortunately, Monty had no patience for a needy five-year-old. He ended us without a word. Just stopped showing up. Then came Tim, the drummer. Julian practically went deaf listening to him practice. Turned out he was trying to deny his sexual preference, so that was that. John, the gambler. Taught Julian poker, blackjack, craps. When a teacher caught Julie working over third graders for their lunch money, I realized I needed to find him a better father figure. Julian found Steven first."

"Another boyfriend?"

"Oh, no. Steven was the youth group leader at church. What a blessing he was."

A "but…" seems imminent, yet Ana is still preoccupied by her memories.

"Please, tell me what was so special about Steven."

Ana blinks, returns to the solarium and me.

"Yes. Yes, of course. Steven. He genuinely liked my son. Took him to ball games, fishing, camping…"

"By himself or with the church group?"

"Both," she answers without hesitation.

Singling out one child for special attention always raises suspicions, but Ana exhibits no reservations, so I choose not to ask.

Yet knowing what Julian just did, how can I not?

"But…?" I hint.

Ana's sharp glance clearly conveys *Not yet*.

She smooths another wrinkle on her hospital gown. "At first, I loved their camping trips, one every summer. Time for myself I'd never had before, right? Heaven! First year, a weekend. Then a week, two weeks. Then when Julian was fourteen—six weeks, when I'd only agreed to three. I was frantic. No cell coverage, no idea where they were. I thought I would never see my son again. I called the church, the police. Then one day they just showed up, acting like nothing was wrong.

"Steven said they were having fun, and he didn't think I wouldn't mind. I told him he was lucky I didn't have him arrested."

"What did he say to that?"

"He promised he would never do anything like it again, but I was still furious. I told him he couldn't see Julian anymore."

"Did you notice any aftereffects? Any changes in Julian?" I still wondered if Steven might have been a pedophile with a preference for young boys.

"Not really. Although it was about that age Julian began to complain about women, especially me. We're ruining the world. Stuff like that. I thought some girl must have embarrassed him—you know how girls that age can be—or maybe it was just hormones messing with his brain."

"Let's skip ahead to this week," I suggest. "Your son didn't carry you a hundred yards into those woods by himself. What happened, and most important, who was Julian working with?"

"In a minute," she stalls again. "You need a little more history."

"Okay."

She grasps her knees, scans the horizon, speaks to the windowpanes. "Julian was never popular in school. Until suddenly he was."

She turns to confront me. "What's the usual reason for that, Ms. Ex-cop?"

"Drugs," I answer honestly. "He was dealing." The same conclusion my father reached.

Ana shuts her eyes hard before facing me again. "It took me way too long to realize that. But yes, I believe Julian was selling marijuana. Probably still is."

"Nothing more dangerous?"

"That I don't know. I like to think not."

"When did you start giving him money?"

"Maybe a year ago. At first, I thought it meant he wasn't dealing anymore, but I don't know that for sure. He just said he was short on rent. Or he needed brakes for his van. Simple things. Things I could justify paying for."

"But…?"

"But lately I thought I heard more tension in his voice. The amounts were higher, too. A thousand dollars, and he wouldn't tell me what it was for."

"That had to worry you."

"Yes. Very much. When he asked for $20,000 in cash, I really got scared. He even said it was a matter of life and death.

"I had the idea that if I delivered it personally he might tell me what was going on, so I held my ground until he agreed. 'Don't use your credit card to get here,' he said, 'No cell phone either.'"

The look on her face begged me to understand. "I love my son, Lauren. More than anything else in the world I want to be part of his life, and Julian a part of mine. I don't expect him to call every day, or even every week. I just need to know if he's happy, or sad, or sick, or hungry, or lonely."

I tell her, "Of course," but I'm considering the significance of her being dragged into the woods. Hiding her there gave Julian and the second man extra time to disappear, but it also risked their being caught right on the spot, especially considering the chair. The temporary comfort had to have been a concession of some sort.

"What can you tell me about the man Julian was with?"

"Not much. He grabbed me and spun me around so fast I never saw his face."

"He was behind you when he injected you with the drug?"

"Yes. And it wasn't long after that that I felt woozy and limp."

"Then let's try a couple easier questions. Was he bigger than Julian? Shorter?"

"Bulkier, I think. Although he had on a rough brown jacket."

"You saw the jacket?"

"Just the sleeve when he put his arm across my collar bone."

"Was he wearing gloves?"

"Yes. Leather ones."

"A hat?"

"I don't know."

"When his arm was across you, was his chin on your head, or was he too tall?"

"Too tall."

"Do you remember any smells? His breath? Maybe something on the jacket?"

"Smoke. The glove and maybe the jacket smelled like cigarettes."

"Okay. Which arm did he use to drag you backwards?"

A slight hesitation. "His right."

"What was his left hand doing?"

"Holding...holding the needle I guess."

"So, he's probably left-handed."

"I guess."

"You're doing great. Now, did he say anything? Anything at all?"

"I remember he told Julian to shut the door. Then maybe a couple more words."

"Did he have an accent? Was his voice high or low? Was it similar to anyone you know?"

"He just sounded bossy. In control. Julian did whatever he was told."

All along, I've wondered whether Julian was being manipulated by someone else. Maybe a close friend who was in trouble got him to pry money out of his mother. Maybe he owed a drug dealer money—or loyalty. Could be a new father figure, or an intimidating bully Julian didn't dare cross.

Whatever the case, the trick will be apprehending whoever it is before he uses Ana's $20,000 to disappear into the ether.

Ana's phone chirps in her pocket.

She lifts it out and reads the screen. The hand holding the phone begins to tremble.

"It's Julian!" She says, as the color drains from her face.

Chapter 36

"SPEAKERPHONE," I WHISPER, before Ana taps the green dot to connect.

"Hi, Ma," says a young man's voice. "Where are you?"

"I'm in the hospital, thanks to you," she retorts. "What's going on? Where are you?"

"Look, Ma. I'm sorry about…about the other night. I never wanted to hurt you, but…but…"

"But what?"

"But my, my partner…well, I couldn't…he…."

"He what? Wanted to kill me?"

"Yes, he did. I'm glad you're okay."

"Okay? I'm in the hospital? Does that sound like I'm okay?"

I pat the air down with both hands trying to make Ana give the kid a chance to talk.

"You're not dead, are you?" Julian retorts without a trace of sympathy.

Uncomfortable with where this seems to be going, I pat the air harder.

Ana takes notice. Gives me a grimace, and rolls her eyes.

"Why did you call, Julie?" She still sounds peeved, but a little less nasty.

"He took it all, Ma. All of it. I'm tapped out again. I'm gonna hafta steal food."

I distract Ana with another hand wave, whisper for her to say she'll call him back.

It's obvious she's about to ignore me, so I shoot her a glare so insistent she does a doubletake.

"Give me a minute," she tells her son. "I'll call you back."

She disconnects and says, "Well…?"

"I get that you're angry. Of course, you are. Me, too. But do we agree that Julian can tell us what the authorities need to catch the bastard who…"

Ana's impatient, "Yes," interrupts me.

"So, isn't our best chance of getting that information right now, when Julian's asking for your help?"

"Again," Ana interjects. "He's asking me again. What do you have in mind?"

I lean forward to talk; she leans forward to listen.

"Why don't you invite Julian to dinner at the Mountain View Café, and let me take care of the rest?"

Ana leans back to give that a sly smile.

Probably hoping to finish with Ana, Officer Cameron is standing expectantly in the doorway.

I would love to hear Ana's next exchange with Julian, but I trust she's capable of getting him to meet us for dinner without me listening in.

As she's placing the call, I usher the officer back into the hallway away from her ears.

I detail my suspicions about Julian, first that he's on the run from something unspecified, second that he's most certainly guilty of taking part in Ana's abandonment Tuesday night and, therefore, possesses information about the second man. I also suspect the places he chose to pick up his mother's money are places he's been before, possibly in the recent past.

"Interesting," Cameron concurs. "Ana insisted on delivering the money he requested in person."

"Yes. She's his mother. She wanted to see him…badly. That was her only stipulation."

"And you think he chose places he's familiar with, places he's been sometime during the last year or two?"

"It's much easier to give directions to someplace you've been, right?"

Cameron rubs his chin.

I couldn't resist the silence. "Ana's arranging for Julian to meet us at the Mountain View Café for dinner tonight. Big surprise, the other guy took the whole twenty thousand for himself. Julian doesn't have a buck to buy himself a bag of Fritos."

Cameron's hazel eyes regard me with even keener interest. "The state of Utah might be willing to feed him for a while," he muses with a smile.

I tell him I think that would be a kindness to society.

"This is a bit above my pay grade," the officer admits. "I'll call my sergeant. He can make it happen."

"Please let us finish our chicken pot pie first, okay? Ana might not see her son again for a while."

Furthermore, before my brand-new, criminal-in-training stepbrother decides to take the words, "You have the right to remain silent," literally, I plan to pry every morsel of information out of him I can get.

Chapter 37

JULIAN IS LATE. The meet was scheduled for 4 p.m., early for the Mountain View Café usuals, but a good time to eat if you haven't had breakfast or lunch.

Ana and I have glasses of iced tea melting in front of us, but I also order a slice of apple pie. It justifies hogging the table better, and I've never had a problem eating dessert first.

The pie is probably from a grocery store freezer, but it was well chosen. I've just dropped my fork back on the plate when a wiry young guy in need of a barber and a laundromat pauses just inside the door. He has a backpack dangling off one shoulder and a haughty expression plastered on his stubbled face. I try to discern a hint of his male parentage, but Julian is too obviously Ana's son—dark wavy hair, olive complexion.

He spots the back of his mother's head, and saunters our way.

When he gets near, Ana pops up as if somebody goosed her. Mixed emotions were racing across her face, but she seems to have settled on angry.

Julian's glance ricochets off his mother to me. "Who the hell are you?"

"She's your stepsister, Julian," Ana intercedes. "Lauren's here because I no longer have a car. But then you already knew that."

There seems to be an electric cable running between them, a thick one conducting enough power to fry any ordinary mortal. Neither seems eager to speak about what's really being exchanged. Not in public. Probably not with me listening either.

"Sit down, Julie."

Ana gestures her son into her side of the booth next to the window, and he complies.

As he's kicking his backpack onto my foot, his head tilts, and a pink, diamondlike stud in his earlobe catches some of the café's tube lighting. My first thought is that Julian has lousy taste in jewelry, but I realize the earring might also have some special significance, like a cherished gift. Either way, it seems contrary to his young, tough-guy persona.

As Ana scooches in beside her son, she flashes me a glance that says, "See? I'm cooperating." Originally, she insisted on sitting across from Julian, but she came around when I explained that me facing Julian suggests I'll be doing most of the talking. It also allows me to run after him, if he suddenly decides to bolt.

A teenage waitress delivers menus, but Julian wants to eat, collect his mother's life savings, and scram. "You have…?" he calls after the girl, but she is intent on delivering coffee, deaf to inconvenient noise. "Bitch!" he says to her retreating back.

"Were you very far away?" I address the young drug dealer, hoping to instill some normalcy to our fraught little meeting.

"Yeh," he admits. "Traffic."

Braxton being relatively close to nothing, this is Julian's first lie. My guess is he was torn about returning here at all, but decided hitting up his mother—again—is the quickest way to solve his current cash problem. Super plus—it also requires the least amount of effort.

Silence reigns for a long moment. But then the waitress returns and we order—two cheeseburgers and fries for Julian, one each for Ana and me.

Mother and Son still don't begin to know how to start talking to each other, which happens to play into my hand perfectly.

Interrogations always start by putting the suspect at ease. You ask about last night's baseball game, the weather forecast, the stage of the moon. Doesn't matter. Eventually, the detainee becomes so bored and pliable he'll talk just to stay awake.

I inquire whether Julian got caught in last night's rain, whether his van is easy on gas, if he's a soccer fan. His one-word answers are uttered with distain, but he's hungry and has nothing to distract him but grunting out a few irritable answers.

Ana maintains a remarkable silence. I can tell she's puzzled, maybe even thinks I've lost my mind. Yet her concentration on the verbal ping-pong game going on before her is so intense, you'd think she bet her life savings on it.

Which I guess is literally true.

When our food arrives, all three of us are glad for the interruption.

I wait for Julian to finish one of his cheeseburgers, then I open my mouth to address him again.

Before I get a word out, he slaps the table with both hands and shouts, "Cut the crap, okay? We're not gonna be best friends."

"Copy that," I agree. "Who was with you on Tuesday night?"

Second cheeseburger already in mid-air, Julian pauses, then slowly returns the sandwich to its plate.

I can't talk about that," he states, accompanied by a look hot enough to slice through steel.

Unfortunately, Ana chooses now to speak. "It's alright, Jules," she interjects, effectively ruining what little finesse I had going with her first words.

"Julian owes you an answer," I retort. "What that man did is unforgiveable."

Julian has now placed clenched fists on either side of his plate. "Butt out, *Lauren.* Why the fuck are you even here?"

"My father sent me to find his wife," I reply reasonably, "and you're lucky as hell I found her. Answer the question, *Julian.* Tell your mother who you were with."

Julian's fists are now quivering. His face is twisted with conflict. He looks at his mother and closes his eyes. "I can't tell you that, Ma."

An agonizing quiet comes over us. Julian lifts his second sandwich, tries to eat, and can't.

"Okay, Julian," I say, trying to cool the air. "Then why don't you tell your mother why you're really here."

The entire café seems to dial down to slow-motion. Julian stares at the mess on his plate. Flexes his fists. He takes a deep breath and turns toward Ana with such powerful intent that his face whiskers appear to stand on end.

"I want to come home, Ma. A few weeks, tops. Just until I sort a few things out."

I half expect Ana to throw up her arms and embrace the kid. To kiss his forehead and hug him to her breast.

She refrains. In fact, she holds perfectly still while she assesses what, to her, must seem like a great gift.

"Whaddya say, Ma?"

An eternity speeds by before she answers.

"You may stay with me until you get back on your feet. But no drugs, Julie. Buying. Selling. *Using.* One sniff of that and you're out on your ear."

"Sure, Ma. No problem."

Gratitude? Nonexistent. Julian falls onto his second cheeseburger like the selfish brat I suspect he has always been.

I pay the bill with Dad's credit card, and we exit the café in a row.

Up ahead, Ana prattles on about how Julian should stay in her motel room tonight; they can set off for Albuquerque in his van tomorrow morning. Their dysfunctional rapport is firmly back in place. Neither one spares me a thought.

I'm not exactly listening to them anyway. We've made it out onto the sidewalk. Ana approaches the street between two parked cars. Julian is one step behind.

I notice three Utah Highway Patrol troopers, aka state police, strategically positioned to intercept us, and cross my fingers hoping Julian doesn't spot them, too.

He does.

Before he can lunge past his mother, I grab the strap of his backpack and tug hard.

He spins toward me, fists flailing.

Kicking him in the balls is a foolish move for oh-so many reasons, and I do know better. Aim is problematic with a moving target. Then you've got your leg right there for him to grab. But I really, really want to do it, so I make the split-second decision to go for it. I've been short on good luck for so long the universe owes me.

Bullseye.

As expected, Julian grasps my outstretched leg. But as we both fall, I hear his prolonged "Ahhhhhh," just before my head bounces off the sidewalk. It hurts like hell, but it is soooo worth it.

Cradling my bleeding head with my hand, I watch a trooper dive on Julian like a defenseman covering a fumbled football. Itching to help, a second officer crowds in, and the scramble ends with Julian in handcuffs.

From the street, Sergeant Broatmarkle, the Utah Highway Patrolman who coordinated the ambush with me on the phone, lifts his chin to acknowledge me. From this distance, I perceive him to be a veteran cop with a businesslike mien and a paunch almost, but not quite, under control.

Now that my leg is free, I stagger upright and look around for Ana.

She is off to the side of the fray, and she is hysterical. While Julian is hauled upright…and read his rights…and patted down up against a cruiser, she twirls and rants and cries.

Soon enough, she and I are left standing on the sidewalk staring at each other. She looks like hell, but for once she doesn't care. Serious life is going on here.

"You did this," she states.

I nod.

She looks away.

"Did you have to?"

I wait a beat to let her remember she could still be tied to a chair in the woods, not to mention dead.

Ana closes her eyes and lowers her head.

"Julian saved me," she tries, lifting her chin and swiping the tears from her cheeks.

I wave my head. "Maybe."

She peers at me again, searching for the source of my doubt.

"We should probably talk about this later," I suggest.

Ana breathes. Does a few mini nods.

Done with Us for now, we turn to watch Sergeant Broatmarkle digging through Julian's backpack. Ostensibly checking for a weapon, his gloved hands carefully place each item he removes into a paper evidence bag.

"Well, lookie this," he exclaims. He has removed the stiff bottom of the backpack, and is now holding a spine-chilling discovery aloft. Joined together like a ponytail are clumps of hair in various colors and lengths, some curly, some straight.

Knowing what the hair trophies mean, I draw in a sharp breath and feel my muscles clench. Surely, the three law-enforcement officers here have the same reaction, for there is only one reason a young man would keep such a collection hidden.

"This a souvenir of some sort, Mr. Tomas?" the sergeant asks. "A little something to remember your conquests?"

Panicked as a man with a gun to his head, Julian is squirming to get free. "That's not mine," he protests, as the officer detaining him tugs his cuffed wrists higher.

Broatmarkle casually holds the evidence aside. "Odd that I found it in your backpack, then."

"It…is…not…mine."

"Then how do you suppose this got here?"

"Somebody put it there." Julian's lips and eyes are wet with emotion. His face damp with sweat.

"Who, Julian? Who do you think put it there?"

"My *father*."

Ana drops to her knees.

"Why? Why would he do that?" Broatmarkle persists.

Wild-eyed, Julian stares at the sergeant for a long moment. Then his shoulders sag and his chin drops to his chest.

As Ana's son is tucked away in the patrol vehicle, the rest of us are helpless to escape a sound that will repeat in our nightmares.

Ana Tomas Beck, rape victim and mother of the accused, is curled up on the ground keening like a dying animal.

Chapter 38

AS ANA GASPS for breath, I tilt her head down between her knees and assure her she'll be okay.

"Broatmarkle," I shout. "Evidence bag!"

Seeing why I need it, he tosses one right away.

Spreading the paper bag open with my fist, I surround Ana's mouth and nose with the opening. Soon, her hyperventilating begins to ease.

Beyond us, the police direct Braxton's modest five o'clock traffic around the cruiser containing Julian Tomas. Another deputy waves gawking pedestrians along on the sidewalk.

I help Ana to her feet, lead her back to the Jeep, and make certain she's comfortable.

She's as dumbstruck and distraught, as anyone who just experienced two horrific shocks could be. The news of Julian being involved with her rapist was enough to ruin all trust. Her son's arrest, yet another staggering blow.

I approach Sergeant Broatmarkle as he finishes a phone call. Up close I take in his bushy, salt-and-pepper eyebrows and prominent nose, the bearing that exudes competence. I pump him for information—where Julian will be taken, and his chances of getting a decent public defender. Stuff Ana will surely want to know.

When we're finished, I drift back to the curb and ask a gentleman with a knowing look whether Braxton has a liquor store.

His eyes narrow as if he's just come face to face with a two-headed zebra.

I repeat my question another way. "I'd like to get some brandy. Where should I go?"

Curling his lips, the man says, "Wyoming?"

The jerk is joking. I can tell because he's laughing to himself as he walks away. He has also answered my question.

I duck into the drug store and buy four chocolate bars instead.

Ana scarcely acknowledges my presence when I climb in and start up the Jeep.

"Seat belt," I remind her.

No response, so I walk around and strap her in myself. Then off we go back to Whispering Pines Motel, because where else would we want to be?

When we arrive, I arrange for us to share a room as far from the office and other guests as possible. The view is of the parking lot, to our left some of the street.

I guide Ana onto the first twin bed and cover her with a blanket. Then I seek out the pregnant maid and bribe her to help me gather our belongings and move them to our new room. She kindly tells me how to find a little-known nook in the office where I can make Ana some hot tea.

We are good for the night.

***

In the morning when we settle in at the Mountain View Café for a late breakfast, it almost feels like home. Ana and I order enough to feed a farmer's family, consume most of it, then linger over yet another coffee refill.

Around us, patrons in workers' garb tuck into eggs and bacon as if calories are of no consequence. Their just-off-a-good-night's-sleep banter is a balm to my nerves. I even catch my breakfast companion giving our waitress a quick smile after she receives another refill. Otherwise, Ana's default expression is Miserably Depressed.

Attempting a normal conversation, I try chatting about my dad. His whiskers in the sink, his childish jokes. I brag about his skill at selling real estate.

Catching on, Ana bemoans his preference for dull colors and baggy jeans. We've each talked to him on the phone, so we know he's in good spirits, concerned by what little we've told him about Julian, but remarkably content for somebody's who's still in the hospital. Of course, his wife has been found, so there's that.

Sensing my stepmother is about as relaxed as she's going to get, I decide it's time to ask the question that's been dangling in the air since yesterday.

"Who is Julian's father, Ana?"

She closes her eyes. When they slowly reopen, they are brimming with tears. She sniffles and grasps the hair above her brow with her fist. She waves her head before looking up from under her arm. When she speaks again, I don't hear the conflict ripping her insides apart. I feel it. The years of agony over my exact question.

"I don't know," she answers just above a whisper. "I can't remember a thing about him."

While she grapples with her truncated memories, I struggle to think how to help her.

Back when I was on the job, I attended a lecture by a forensic hypnotist. It both fascinated and amazed me, especially since the procedure ensures that whatever the hypnosis reveals can be used in a court of law.

My internal debate leans toward no. What if remembering the rape traumatizes Ana all over again to no useful end?

I charge our breakfast and leave a tip. Then we step out into crisp mountain air fragrant with pine sap, restaurant exhaust, and dust. Overhead, white clouds with dove-gray underbellies stand out against the intense blue of the sky. Birds tweet in the bushes. A car with an open window rolls slowly by, allowing us to hear a wife patiently tell her husband, "No, dear. First the dry-cleaner, then the grocery…"

Everything reassuringly normal—except to Ana.

I tell her there may be a way for her to help Julian after all. "If you could tell the authorities who his father is, wouldn't that go a long way toward exonerating Julian?"

Ana halts only inches from where her son was apprehended the night before. "But how…?"

"Hypnosis sometimes works," I hint with a healthy dose of doubt.

Ana's teeth clench. Her shoulders stiffen. She is more than conflicted, she is frightened to her core, and I completely get it. Why would anyone want to remember something like that?

Unless…

Unless the son you adore claims his father framed him for raping and killing multiple young women—and you believe him.

While we drive back to the motel, Ana's silence resembles a trance. Only when I've parked in front of our room does she finally emerge from wherever she's been.

"I have to try, don't I?" she says simply. "For Julian. For all those poor girls. So, yes. I'll try it."

I'm grasping the steering wheel hard enough to hurt my hands.

"You're sure?" I press.

"How do we start?" she inquires, and the conviction in her voice forces me to dismiss my own doubts.

"I guess I make a call."

Ana gives me a sharp nod, and reaches for the Jeep's door handle.

Once inside our room, she flops onto the newly made bed and waves me away. Exhausted and full of comfort food, she will sleep until lunch.

I step outside with my cell phone, notice the Jeep offers the only seating in sight, and settle myself on the passenger's side to google forensic hypnotists.

There are a handful of possibilities, but, unfortunately, I don't recognize any of the names. Since my call will be coming pretty much out of the blue, I hoped to contact the man whose lecture left such an impression. Then I could at least mention that I heard him speak.

Scarp is back from his honeymoon and nearing his lunch break at work. He sounds just as pleased to see my name on his screen as he was the last time I phoned.

"Dammit, Lauren. What is it now?"

I explain that my new stepbrother has possibly been framed for multiple murders by his father. Then I ask if he knows how to get in touch with the hypnotist we heard.

"No, I do not. And I can't believe you're serious about this."

"Sorry. I just don't know what else to do."

Scarp snorts. I can almost see him wave his head with disbelief.

"Put another way, just get me the guy's name, and I'll find him myself. There can't be that many forensic hypnotists around."

"Like about a hundred in the whole country." Scarp's tone is *Gotcha* heavily doused with *You are a gargantuan pain in the ass.*

We have little more to say. Just "Text me. Please!" and "Yeah, right."

Half an hour later, I'm still staring out the Jeep's windshield wondering what's next if this, admittedly desperate, notion doesn't pan out.

I'm so far gone into my head that the ding from my cell phone makes me jump.

Scarp's text reads, "Geoffrey Palmer. Don't call me back."

The Internet is a marvel.

By the time Ana awakens from her morning nap, I've checked us out of the motel, left a goodbye tip for the pregnant maid, and loaded the Jeep with all our belongings.

Chapter 39

"WHERE ARE WE GOING?" Ana asks, jumpy and flustered by my animation and the sudden exit from the motel.

"Salt Lake Cityish," I reply, for we're headed toward a suburb I hope I can find in time.

Bless his heart, Geoffrey Palmer, the certified forensic hypnotist I found so fascinating, answered on the second ring with, "Palmer here. How can I help you?"

Our conversation slid downhill from there.

Palmer was neither willing nor able to hypnotize Ana. Main problem: he lives in Chicago. Also, we can't afford him. Otherwise, he was as useful as he could be from afar for free.

Specifically, he pointed out that I do not need incontrovertible evidence to start getting Julian off the hook and out of jail. What I need is a name. Or, failing that, a detailed description of Ana's rapist. The presently employed police can then work on locating the actual perpetrator, checking his and Julian's alibis against any hair sample matches, etcetera.

Toward that end, Dr. Palmer told me in general terms how to plumb Ana's memory for whatever she's been repressing about her rapist's identity.

He did not seem optimistic about my chance of success. However, he did wish me luck and requested a report. "If you don't mind. This is a first for me."

"Where are we going?" Ana asks.

"It takes a little explaining," I hedge.

Ana sighs, and I drive a little faster.

"We're going to see a hypnotist."

"Seriously? You already got an appointment?"

"Yes."

Ana relaxes a notch. "So, what's the problem?"

Might as well spell it out.

"The hypnotist we're going to see works for a circus. Correction. He owns a circus. He's the most popular act."

A glance reveals that Ana has turned red from her hairline down.

"Now before you get too bent out of shape, I did speak with a certified forensic hypnotist, one of very few in the country, and he gave me an...an outline on how to question you when...when the man we're going to see puts you under. Dr. Palmer said if there's anything worthwhile for you to share, there's a chance it will emerge."

Ana actually laughs. "Good God," she mutters to herself.

We locate an array of circus vehicles in a grocery store parking lot on the outskirts of a sparse suburb of a suburb of Salt Lake City. The vehicles are trucks and campers painted in Harold's Fun-for-All Circus's signature blue labeled with silver and gold script. As before, not a caged animal in sight. Not even a stray dog wandering around. I knock on the door of the camper nearest to where I park and ask a wizened man with a pink moustache where I might find Harold.

Spud, for that is the name he gives when we shake hands, directs me to another camper at the far edge of the group.

"Thank you," I say graciously.

"If you say so," Spud replies as he shuts his door.

I shrug for Ana's benefit, and she waves her head. Her attitude about all this has become very hard to read.

I've already told her everything I know about the process, but for the fourth time I ask if she is really up for it.

"If you say so," she replies, but her lips twitch and her eyes crinkle, so I assume she's still willing.

I remind her that she may never be able to forget what she remembers during her induction. "Does that worry you?"

Ana's forehead creases. "Not as much as Julian going to prison for something he didn't do."

Focusing on that goal allows me to believe my plan isn't as cockamamie as Geoffrey Palmer made it sound. It just depends on Harold's skill and what, if anything, Ana allows herself to remember.

I put on a smile and knock on the indicated camper door.

As he gestures us inside with a sweep of his hand, the hypnotist's seamed face is flushed with joy. Indeed, his whole body vibrates with excitement. His hair is a wild floss of whitening blond, his eyebrows wiry and unkempt. He's wearing a Madras plaid shirt with a missing button and jeans stretched to a comfortable sag.

Out of the corner of my eye I notice a satin ringmaster's top hat on a corner table. In general, the place is pretty threadbare, with worn Formica surfaces and the fragrance of sausage in the air. On a hook in the hallway a red jacket embellished with gold braid is surely absorbing the aroma from the frying pan in the sink.

"I'm Lauren Beck, and this is your client, Ana Beck," I relate.

Harold's thick lips widen to reveal a gleaming set of purchased teeth.

"Pleased to meetcha," he replies, his brown eyes devouring Ana.

"May I speak to you a moment outside?" I ask the circus owner.

Harold spares me a look.

"Sure. Why not?"

He offers an outstretched hand for Ana to gently grasp. Then he leads her to the padded bench serving as a sofa and waits until she takes a seat.

Ana's pink cheeks tell me she's charmed by the gentlemanly gesture. It is patently clear which of us will be asking her the tough questions.

"Be right back," I tell her, and she flutters her eyelashes in my direction.

Outside I fill Harold in on my conversation with Geoffrey Palmer, describing in detail how he recommended we handle Ana's "induction." I also give him a short history of Ana's relationship with her son.

"So please be super careful," I conclude.

The circus owner responds with a series of um-humms and yep-yeps. "No problem," he finally answers using words. "Used to do psychological hypnotics," he remarks. "Troubled people. Too many troubled people. A circus act is much more fun."

He looks me in the eye to make sure I've gotten the message.

I have exhaled, I realize. I have also lowered my shoulders, which had crept almost up to my ears.

"So, you've got this," I remark.

"Not necessarily," he admits. "Why don't I put her under, and when she's ready, you feed me your questions."

"I'll be recording the session on my phone. To...to show the police, if it comes to that."

"Okay. So, whisper your questions. You're not going to hold the phone with your mouth, are you?"

"Uh, no."

"Then let's get started. I gotta grocery shop when we're done."

Thinking of his tiny home, a hint of skepticism may have crossed my face.

"For everybody," he amends. "The cook has to take her kid to a dentist. She's my ex-wife, by the way."

"Oh! Lonely at the top?"

"You have no idea." He gestures toward Ana with his shoulder. "She single by any chance?"

"No!" I exclaim. "She's married to my father."

Harold's grin is a little lewd. "Lucky man."

He waves me back inside.

Chapter 40

HAROLD BEGINS BY kissing Ana's hand. He also looks deeply into her, admittedly beautiful, eyes and asks her a couple calming questions. "Where do you live, dear?" "Does your husband treat you well?" "Too bad," he retorts to her affirmative answer with that lewd, yet playful, smile.

He has pulled a single chair over to be level with his subject. I'm left standing with my cell phone trained on Ana's face.

A glance at Harold's profile assures me he was dead serious about his psychological hypnosis work and is equally serious about what he's doing right now. I feel a slight tingle in the hand holding the phone recording this, a nervous frisson of anticipation.

Soon the hypnotist's voice becomes monotone and repetitive. He suggests Ana imagine her favorite place of relaxation. "You're there now. Paint the picture in your mind. That's it. Feel how serene it is. Relax. So restful. Breathe slowly…That's it. Now focus on your eyes blinking. Relax... Now look upward. When I count to five, your eyes will close…"

He spares a glance at me and nods. I admit I'm feeling pretty relaxed myself.

After some more repetition, Harold seems satisfied that Ana is into her subconscious enough for a test.

"You just put your hand in a bucket of ice," he suggests.

Ana's hand jerks up and shakes off imaginary water.

Harold reaches out and pinches the same hand.

No reaction.

"You're doing great, Sweetie," he coos. "Now if you ever feel uncomfortable, just raise your index finger.

"Okay, now. Your name is Ana Tomas Beck and you live in Albuquerque, New Mexico. Right?"

Ana nods.

Harold looks to me for a question.

"Son's name?" I whisper.

Harold asks.

"Julian," the doting mother replies with a brief smile.

We repeat the whisper/ask routine with simple stuff. How old is Julian? What do you do for a living? Where did you grow up? After Ana answers the latter with the name of a village in Mexico, I start feeding the questions that need to be asked.

"Who is Julian's father, Ana?"

"Danny. The boy who raped me." she answers with a scowl, and I nearly drop my phone.

"Can you tell me his last name?"

I hold my breath while she pauses to think. "I don't know," she finally answers. "I don't think he mentioned it."

"How old was Danny then, Ana?"

Her forehead wrinkles. "Older than me. He was already out of school."

"What else can you tell me about him?"

"He's very tall and strong."

"Can you see his face?"

A nod.

"What color are his eyes?"

"Blue. Pale blue."

"Hair?"

"Brown. Medium brown. A little curly."

"Let's go back to the day he raped you. Exactly what happened? Take your time…"

"Danny met me after school. We'd talked a few times before, and I liked him. I thought he was going to drive me home."

"He had a car?"

"No, an old pickup."

"Color?"

"I don't know. It was muddy."

While she shifts back and forth on the bench, I watch her right index finger. So far, it hasn't moved.

"Go on...you're in his truck..."

"Yeah. He turned toward me and said, 'You don't really want to go home, do you?' When I didn't answer, he just smiled, and that made me laugh. We drove about a mile out of town, then he parked on a tractor lane between two avocado fields. He pulled me close and started kissing me, but pretty soon he got rough, ripping at my clothes and grabbing. I slapped at his arms and tried to push him away, but he yanked me out of the truck and threw me on the ground."

She tells us more, much more, and when she stops for breath, I realize I've been holding mine.

"What else do you remember about that day?" Harold asks on my behalf.

"I scratched his face bad," Ana admits. "He bled all over my blouse. I was a total mess. On the walk home, I had to hide if a car came by. Then I had to wait outside until I could sneak past my mother and change."

"Did you tell anyone about the rape? A friend or a priest?"

A vigorous headshake. "Nobody. I felt stupid and ashamed. When I started showing, my father went crazy. He was angrier than I'd ever seen him. He wanted to throw me out, but my mother said keeping the baby would be punishment enough, so that's what happened."

"To your knowledge, have you ever seen Danny again?"

Ana appears to be thinking. "No," she answers. Then another more forceful, "No."

The index finger lifts, and my disappointment feels like a heavy weight.

"You're slowly going to wake up now, Ana," Harold tells his subject, "...and this is important. When you're awake, you will remember everything we discussed. Understand?"

Calmer now, Ana says, "Yes."

"Good. Your eyes are beginning to open. Your breathing is normal. You're totally relaxed. You will forget nothing...

"When I count to five you will awaken and remember everything we've discussed...One, two, three, four, five..."

Ana rouses as if from a brief power nap. She blinks her eyes hard, and looks from Harold to me.

"How'd I do?" she asks.

In unison, we tell her, "Great!"

"Now for the hard part," Harold announces. "We go over all of it with you awake."

It takes another twenty minutes, but it all comes out— Danny with the pale blue eyes and curly, medium brown hair, and all the rest.

"Remind you of anyone you've seen lately?" Harold presses when other questions have been exhausted.

Ana stares off into the distance, begins to reply, then stops.

"You said you scratched his face. Could that have left a scar?"

Ana's eyes widen. Her body shudders.

Both Harold and I know better than to say a word. We scarcely breathe.

"He has a beard now," Ana remarks with little indication of the turmoil that must be roiling inside.

"Who does, Ana?" I prompt.

"Steven," she says, as her hand shields her eyes. "Steven Stockhardt from church."

The youth group volunteer who befriended Julian when he was about ten or eleven.

"Why didn't I recognize him before?" Ana's gaze fixes on me, but she's really asking herself.

"Trauma, my dear," Harold replies. "Perfectly natural," he adds, and I recognize the professional pride he possessed—before the traumas his previous subjects piled onto him became too much to bear.

Ana's attention slides onto the circus owner's face, and their expressions seem to mesh.

Confident that I'm not needed, I step outside the trailer to process my own thoughts.

Chapter 41

OUTSIDE THE CIRCUS owner's trailer, the sky is evenly clouds and clarity, which strikes me as about right.

So much has fallen into place, I can scarcely contain my relief. Not just that Ana managed to identify her rapist. The rest, too. My imagination buzzes with possibilities.

Yet before I get too carried away, I phone Sergeant Broatmarkle with the names.

"Com'on. The woman's had amnesia for years," he exclaims. "How'd you get that?"

"With a little help from a friend," I hedge. "Danny, now known as Steven Stockhardt, was a church youth group leader when Julian was eleven." I give him the church name and location, then mention that Stockhardt rented a room from a female congregant, "but not very recently."

"Whoa, there. You've gotta give me more than that."

"That's all she wrote, Sergeant. And you're welcome. Bye!"

I lower myself to the dusty ground and rest my back against Harold's camper. A puffy cloud is drifting by, and it's giving me a lovely Zen vibe. I stretch out my legs and drop my arms to my sides.

"Danny" drove a muddy pickup truck, "his" truck Ana said under hypnosis. If true, that made him old enough to drive and employed enough to afford the truck. He took her to a spot between two avocado fields, which—theoretically—explained the mud and perhaps a farming-related occupation. Since she said she never saw him again after the rape, it's possible he moved on shortly thereafter.

Pulling a piece of grass from the clump beside me, I twiddle it between my fingers.

What was Stockhardt's endgame? What did he actually do?

He cultivated a relationship with Julian, that's what. So he must have learned about Ana's son from family or friends, local people he knew back in Mexico. Both culturally and calendar-wise, there would have been no question. The child had to be his.

Fast forward. Even if Stockhardt's original village contacts lost sight of Ana and her son, Ana's sister still lives there. Maybe he sweet-talked her into revealing Ana's latest location. After all, he's smooth enough to convince church people he's good with children.

Just as I'm beginning to wonder what Ana and Harold have been talking about for so long, my phone alerts me to a text message from Broatmarkle. "Julian arraigned," it says. "Bail denied. Talk tomorrow." And we will, as promised.

I thank the sergeant for the news, just as Ana emerges from the trailer.

She appears to be a shaken, but satisfied, customer. Stroking the hand Harold holds to help her to the ground, she gazes at him with a mixture of gratitude, pain, and perhaps some degree of relief.

I hop to my feet and dust off my bottom. Pay Harold with a personal check marked, "Thanks a million." Shake his hand warmly and wish him well.

"What now?" Ana asks after Harold scurries off to grocery shop.

I show her Broatmarkle's message, then pause to let the information sink in.

"You hungry?" I ask. I've noticed a flashing sign for pizza immediately inside the grocery store whose parking lot houses Harold's circus.

"Not really, but I guess we should eat."

We settle into a roped off dining area with pepperoni slices and Diet Cokes.

Considering what she's been through, Ana seems remarkably mellow. I guess the hypnosis might have something to do with it, but it might be as simple as getting an answer to the question that plagued her for nineteen years.

"Why would Steven do that?" Ana ponders. "Get in touch with Julian?"

"Curiosity, ego, flirting with danger," I speculate. "Probably not fatherly love."

"No," she agrees. "Probably not. Will giving the police Steven's name really get Julian released?"

"Not right away," I answer honestly. "But sure. They'll have to match the hair samples to victims, then check where Julian was at the time of the crimes. But, yes, if he's innocent, I think he'll get out from under that."

I share a related thought. "Since Julian isn't going anywhere for a while, how about renting a car so you can pick up Dad and take him home?" Cheryl the Nurse's generosity, though vast, shouldn't be imposed upon any longer than necessary.

Ana seems to breathe for the first time in days. "I *would* rather take care of him myself."

"Smart move," I concur.

And, just like that, I breathe more freely, too. Removing Dad and Ana from my To Do list shifts me off daughter duty and fully back into cop mode.

"What will you do?" Ana inquires.

"Oh, I'll stick around awhile. See how things work out."

Why give the woman something new to worry about?

Chapter 42

WITH ANA HEADING south toward Cheryl Anderson's home and my father, I head back toward Broatmarkle's Utah Highway Patrol barracks, which are also a reasonable distance from the detention center where Ana's son is being held.

At a rest stop I reach the sergeant by phone, and after we iron out the details of our morning meeting with Julian, I fess up about the hypnosis. Broatmarkle almost lays an egg, but since he already discovered the Steven Stockhardt name is fishy, he really shouldn't complain.

"Want Harold's number?" I tease. "Maybe you'll need him sometime."

Never mind his response.

I also text Julian's assigned lawyer to alert him that his client's father probably did plant the hair trophies in the backpack. I also tell him about the hypnosis. What the defense attorney chooses to do with the information is up to him.

A quick internet search secures me a room in a B&B. Turns out it smells like gingersnaps and is adorned with Wild West memorabilia and lace. Better yet, the three other breakfast guests are so wound up about their upcoming day that I'm spared talking about mine.

The detention center's meeting room couldn't be less welcoming. Bland two-tone walls contain the usual rectangular table with Julian and his lawyer seated across from the bulky sergeant and me. I trust a recording device is in operation.

The lawyer is a harried man in a limp brown suit. He wears rimless glasses that slip down his narrow nose and frequently require poking back into place. Mr. Demming is his name, and I met his Pennsylvania counterparts dozens of times. Each was universally overworked and driven, but their competence spanned a wide range. Since I personally believe Julian to be guilty of much more than his mother's ordeal, I haven't nudged Ana to hire a lawyer of her own choosing. Why not wait and see if spending the money becomes necessary?

For me, apprehending Julian's father takes precedence over anything else.

This information-seeking event is aimed at exactly that. Sergeant Broatmarkle will preside, possibly watched over by a rep from the Utah State Bureau of Investigations or a Utah Amber Alert Investigation Component Coordinator, whoever got snagged to come listen in on short notice. I can't see who's behind the one-way window, but I sense the invited parties' hunter instincts bristling back there. I'm pretty wired myself.

Even washed up, Julian looks derelict, but I may be projecting. He twitches from lack of drugs or nerves, and he meets no one eye to eye. Were it up to him, I'm sure he would bolt out the door and disappear. I don't blame him. Not for that anyway.

That said, I also acknowledge a lot of ruined youthful potential that isn't entirely his fault. When your dad's a rapist, you are not off to a very good start.

Broatmarkle clears his throat and says, "Shall we?"

Demming nods with closed eyes, giving the impression he wouldn't mind following Julian out the door.

"Believe it or not, Julian...do you mind me addressing you as Julian?" The kid flares his nose, so the sergeant sucks in a breath and continues. "We're here to try to help you, son. In other words, whatever you say that helps us helps you. Understood?"

Julian's mouth slants down toward the left. His dark eyes seek out a blank spot on the wall.

"All right then. What can you tell us about Steven Stockhardt?"

Waiting for this meeting, Broatmarkle admitted there is scarcely any information about such a person in the southwest. A driver's license issued in New Mexico; a DUI citation in Wyoming; a Salt Lake City, Utah, post office box listed as a mailing address. No passport. No vehicle. In Albuquerque, Steven did rent a room from an elderly widow he met at church, but someone else is living there now. Yet it's the name Julian knows, so it will have to do.

When asked how he learned that Mr. Stockhardt was his father, sweat actually breaks out on Julian's stubbled face. Yet he answers the sergeant willingly, speaking almost as if they're the only two here.

"The camping trip when I was thirteen. We talked about all sorts of things. Women. Girls," a short 'heh' regarding the latter. "Steve likes girls more than women." Julian lifts his eyes to see how his teenage naughtiness goes over with the older man.

"Why's that, Julian? Did he explain?"

Julian performs a puzzled blink. "They're not tainted yet," as if it's obvious. "'The devil hasn't led them astray.'"

"What else did he 'teach' you on that trip? How to collect hair trophies perhaps?"

The lips tilt again. "Wouldn't you just love to know?"

Broatmarkle ignores the bait. "Did he at any time admit that he raped your mother?"

"Naw, nothin' like that," Julian answers easily. "They had an affair was all. Sure, she was young, but he was, too."

Approximately nineteen was Ana's estimate, which made Stockhardt about thirty-nine now. Twenty years of freedom to do as he pleased.

Broatmarkle circles his hand to suggest all of Julian's present problems. "Let's go back to the beginning of all this. Did Stockhardt ask you to press your mother for money, or did you offer?"

"Steve asked."

"Okay, and what were the circumstances."

Julian wobbled back and forth sideways. "He said he was in a bit of a jam."

"What did you think that meant, 'in a bit of a jam?'"

"Something about a girl. Her dad was after him. Something like that. He needed to get out of town for a while. I offered him a couple bucks, but he just laughed. Then he asked if maybe my mother was good for a loan."

"A loan?"

"Well, not a loan. Just a hit, you know."

"Like kids do with their mother."

"Yeah, like that."

"So, what did you say?"

"About the ask? I said sure, why not? He was my dad, you know? What was I supposed to say?"

"All in the family, right?"

"Exactly."

"When did his demands get really serious?"

Julian appeared to think. "About the third time, I guess. He wasn't just fishing anymore, you know?"

"Seeing what he could get."

"Right. That time he was dead serious."

"Did he scare you, Julian?"

"Yeah. I guess you could say that." Julian's gaze suddenly drops to his hands.

"So, in return, you scared your mother."

Julian's eyes snap back to Broatmarkle. "You bet I did. Like I said, Steve was dead serious."

"Okay. Got it. So now you've got your mother up here at the motel ready to meet you. Tell us about that."

"Oh, man. Do I have to?"

"Yes, Julian. You do."

So far, Demming might as well have been asleep. Now he touches Julian's arm and whispers in the kid's ear. Probably reminding him not to incriminate himself.

Which the sergeant perceives. "Just tell us what Stockhardt did, Julian. Can you do that?"

"Yeah. Yeah, I guess. He gave Ma an injection. Then he made me look for the money—which he took," Julian adds with bitterness.

"Then what?"

"He made me help him carry Ma into the woods."

"When you got there, what did you think would happen next?"

"I thought he was going to kill her, but…but I talked him out of it. I told him to go, that I'd do it."

"And what did he say to that?"

Julian suddenly looks conflicted. "He said he was proud of me. That he knew I could do it."

He had been speaking to the table, but now he faces Broatmarkle and me head on.

"But I didn't do it. I saved her life. You guys know I did." He glances at us one by one while Demming closes his eyes and nods.

I'm finding this difficult to watch, Julian honestly believing he did something good.

Demming finally chimes in. "Suppose my client helps you locate Mr. Stockhardt, what will you do for him?"

"We've still got hair trophies found in Julian's possession."

"My client insists they were planted. Assuming that proves to be true, what can you do for Mr. Beck?"

We'll go easy, counselor," Broatmarkle replies, "if that's what you mean."

"Drop charges easy? Or just recommend a lighter sentence?"

The sergeant waffles. "Not entirely up to me. His mother was in grave danger, and he was the one who put her there."

Unfazed and almost disinterested, Demming pretends to do his job. "And how do you expect my client to accomplish this feat, Sergeant? Eh? All you've got is a man who uses aliases and moves around just as any repeat criminal would. If you've got nothing better to do than badger this young man for information he obviously doesn't have, I think this meeting is over."

Whoa. What happened to the original premise: Everybody trying to enlist Julian's help so they can help him?

I lift my hand.

All three men swivel to stare at me.

I focus on the one immediately to my right.

"Can we speak privately for a minute?" I ask the sergeant.

Chapter 43

ALONE OUTSIDE THE INTERVIEW room with Broatmarkle, I explain how Julian can trap his father by offering enough cash to leave the country for good. I also point out that Stockhardt has no way of knowing Julian is in custody, or that Ana is still alive.

"You can trace his location with the phone call, right?"

The Utah state police sergeant's sizeable nose squeezes into some serious, bad-smell wrinkles.

"Com'on," I urge. "It'll be good for us, and good for Julian."

Broatmarkle clicks his tongue and waves his head. "This is the stepbrother you've known exactly five minutes?"

"Yep."

"The one you set up to get arrested?"

"When you put it that way..."

Crossing my fingers behind my back, I explain my readjusted Plan B.

Broatmarkle considers. "I checked into you, you know."

"And...?"

"Sorry about...about the cancer thing. Good to see you're okay."

"Thanks."

"Heard some homicide dick thinks you're a pain in the ass."

"Oh?"

His lips twitch. "Same thing they say about me."

"We're good then?"

He sniffs and slowly lifts his chin toward the trees. "So, this notion of yours…"

"Whaddya think?"

He leans his big head toward his even bigger shoulder. "Don't have much choice, do we?"

His twinkling eyes suggest sarcasm, and he's right. If my plan fails, Stockhardt will have an even greater incentive to disappear into the wind.

However, the opposite is also correct. Without another card up our sleeve, the only thing left is to bluff.

Stuffing one hand in his pocket, Broatmarkle opens the interview room door with the other.

I follow him back in.

"You got a way to contact your dad?" he asks Julian even before we sit down.

Julian's left eyebrow raises.

Twenty minutes later I'm back in the interview room with Julian. A strong guard is watching over us. Demming the Lawyer and Broatmarkle the Cop are now hidden behind the one-way glass. This morning's other investigators took a break and may return for Julian's actual performance. If there is one.

As usual, I'm sizzling with adrenaline and determination but don't dare show it. At this point, feral cats are more trusting than my stepbrother.

"You again," Julian says with the expected disgust.

I deposit a brown paper box containing a cheeseburger, fries, and a soda between his two closed fists.

"Why's your dad been trying to kill me?" I wonder aloud as I gracefully alight onto the opposite chair.

Julian's hands stop before the burger meets his mouth. "How the hell should I know? You probably pissed him off."

"Never met the guy, Julie," I retort, using the despised endearment his mother uses. Since sweetness and light are never going to happen between us, mutual annoyance is much more in character.

Julian smirks. "Then why'd he try to kill you?"

Since that was my question, I suppose it is also my answer. Daddy didn't do it.

Nuts, another dead end.

I let that sit a minute.

"You're in deep shit," I remind the detainee. "Your father framing you for his crimes? Not nice. We're talkin' major prison time. Not nice at all. Then, of course, you're here, and he's…" I flutter my fingers like a flying bird.

I lean partway across the table as if to confide. "What if I told you there's a way you can get out from under and put your troubles where they belong—on him."

Julian appears to be giving the corner of lettuce that slipped out of the hamburger bun more thought than my remark. While he eats—so slowly he's either passive aggressive or really tired of cheeseburgers—I cross my fingers in the hope he'll come onboard.

By the time the last French fry is gone, Steven Stockhardt's kid looks exhausted. I want to feel sorry for him, but my foot can't find the first rung of that particular ladder.

However, I should at least try to meet him halfway.

"You had good times with your dad?" I hint.

A nod.

"Maybe until he started pressing you for big money?"

Julian crumbles the burger wrapper and drops it into the empty box. Eventually, he meets my eyes.

"I bet it was around the time that newspaper article about your mom came out. If he googled her and saw it, he probably figured there was more money to be had."

Julian's stare intensifies.

I toss a hand. "No choice. You had to hit her up for whatever you could get."

Julian looks away, but I keep talking.

"Your mom loves you a lot, you know. Otherwise, why insist on delivering the money in person? She misses you. She wanted to see for herself that you're okay."

A grudging, "Yeah, maybe."

"I guess you realize as soon as Stockhardt got his hands on the money, both of you became expendable."

Julian's blinking suggests my assumption is wrong. Whatever the reason, he still needs to believe he's bulletproof with regard to his father, a delusion it might be best to preserve right about now.

I back off with a digression. "Before I forget, is Steven Stockhardt your dad's real name?"

Julian rustles in his chair. "Why wouldn't it be?"

His deflection makes me think the kid might have a clue after all.

Which prompts another idea Broatmarkle and the others will probably hate.

And yet maybe. Just maybe…

My back is to the observers, so I write a hasty note. Show it to Julian, then tear the page off the pad.

While I ask aloud if there's anything he wants to say to his mom, I slide the slip of paper under the other pages. If I could get away with eating it, I would.

Julian's eyes squint as if he can't quite figure out what I want.

I mouth silently, "Make up something," and tap the notepad with the pencil eraser.

He's staring at my hand, so I expose the hidden page ever so slightly with my thumb.

Finally catching on, Julian mumbles, "Uh, tell her I'm sorry."

I shoot him a grin and write that down.

"What else? Your mom's a good cook. Anything you especially miss?" I wave him on with my free hand.

"Paella. Yeah. Tell her that. I miss her paella."

I jot another note. "I can't spell paella. Here. You write it."

I slide the pad across the table and offer him the pencil.

Julian reads what is now on the top page, accepts the offered pencil, and gives me another open-mouthed stare.

I widen my eyes and perform the tiniest of nods.

With one final hope-you-know-what-you're-doing eye roll, Julian jots down his answer.

***

An hour and a half later the burner phone Julian had on him when he was arrested has been charged, and a call trace is ready to go. A beefy guard stands by outside the interview room. Demming the Lawyer, Broatmarkle, and whoever else came back to observe are behind the one-way window with a recorder running. I wager not one of us is anywhere close to optimistic about this.

On the bright side, Julian exudes youthful energy and an almost disturbing eagerness. Were I to guess, the rewards Broatmarkle and I outlined to incentivize him offered both relief and hope, each non-existent since the day Steven Stockhardt started pressuring him for cash.

"Speakerphone," I remind Julian before he places the call, and I have to remain silent. I've got my pad and pencil on standby in case I need to suggest anything during the critical conversation, but I'm praying I won't need to intervene. One unnatural hesitation on Julian's part could spook Stockhardt and cause him to hang up.

My stepbrother pokes a final button, and my hands begin to sweat.

"Julian?" a male voice responds to the audible ring.

"Yeah, dad. Who else?"

"You shouldn't have called, kid. Goodbye."

"Wait! I've got news."

The click of Stockhard's disconnect punches the air out of all of us.

Chapter 44

SO FAR SO GOOD, I think when Stockhardt hangs up. It means he got my text.

While I'm trying not to look pleased, Broatmarkle flashes a glance my way. His shaggy left eyebrow rises, and I worry that he smells a rat.

Neither of us says anything, however. Not while Julian is escorted out by the guard. Not while Demming silently hustles past us in the hall, off to help another poor sap. Or not, as the case may be.

Broatmarkle and I migrate to the lockup's front entrance along with the two higher-ups and share limp-handed thanks and farewells.

"Waste of my time," one mutters.

"And money," the second concurs.

We lowerlings sigh with relief when the specialists reach their cars.

Finally alone at the top of three cement steps, arms folded across our waists, we take a moment to stare up at an appropriately gray sky.

When Broatmarkle suddenly switches his hands to his hips and turns to me, I brace myself for a browbeating.

"How'd you do it?" The question doubles as an accusation.

I draw in breath and glance up at a treetop. "I…uh…um…."

"Out with it, Beck. That perp was warned. Had to be you. How'd you do it?"

"Already you don't trust me?"

He gives me The Stare.

Busted.

I rock back and forth on my heels. Wrinkle my nose. Tell him, "Julian has a second number for Stockhardt."

"Oh?"

"Yep. One exclusive to them." When I googled disposable feature phones, I found some that only do calls and text. Apparently, they have an extra-long battery life if you don't use them much. Or you can get yourself a camp stove that charges electronics, if you happen to be hiding out in the woods.

Broatmarkle inhales enough air to fill a bellows, then slowly lets it out. "You guessed," he says. Two words, but a tome's worth of implied recriminations. "We've got a major repeat offender here—and you *guessed*."

"I've got an emergency contact. Bet you do, too."

"It's a little different for a rapist."

"I get that. Loner. Plans to disappear. But as far as Stockhardt knows, Julian killed his own mother to help him get away. Even if you were headed for parts unknown, wouldn't you keep an emergency resource like that in your pocket?"

"Yeah. Sure. But bottom line—you guessed!"

"I made an assumption. Then I asked Julian if the phone existed when I slipped him a note."

"Humph." The sergeant lifts his pointy chin in order to peer down his nose.

"The paella bit was bullshit, right?" he remarks, as if it's the answer to a question in his head. "And you, what? Called the perp?"

"Oh, please. Do I sound like a nineteen-year-old male? I texted the guy."

"…and you took this risk on your own because…?"

"Because I wouldn't believe it if Julian said he got wealthy all of a sudden, and I didn't think Stockhardt would buy it either. It'd be like turning over a straight-flush before the last chip hits the table."

Broatmarkle exhales again, this time with exasperation. "You risked any chance of catching a serial rapist/killer."

I wave my head. "I don't think so. I've been in this almost from the beginning, and I think I've got it right."

"Maybe you don't."

"I think I do."

"You should have told me."

"I wanted you to react like everybody else."

He shows me a disgusted, frustrated face, the perfect response to Stockhardt hanging up—and to me right now.

Properly chastised, I promise not to do it again.

Broatmarkle grunts, then asks what I said in the text. "Speaking as Julian, of course…"

"Of course."

"I said I was on a borrowed phone because cops were monitoring my cell. If he, Stockhardt, got a call on our exclusive number, he should answer, but 'hang up quick and move,' which Stockhardt obviously did."

"Obviously." Broatmarkle remains both sarcastic and peeved.

I pretend not to notice. "When Julian calls again, Stockhardt's supposed to ask about me. If Julian uses the code word 'bitch,' it's safe for them to talk."

Nothing fancy, but beautifully functional, if I do say so myself. If the rest of the plan works, I may have to stitch *'hang up quick and move'* onto a pillow.

For Broatmarkle, the operative word in all that was, "If." He snorts, surprises me by clamping his left hand on my shoulder, then glares into my soul.

"What?" I ask.

"You need my help."

"I'm counting on it. Yes."

"Gutsy move, Lauren Louise. I'll give you that."

I assume that doesn't require an answer.

My new partner sighs and lowers his large frame onto the topmost cement step. Looking up, he says, "Talk to me, Lauren Beck."

I join him a companionable distance away.

Then I tell him everything else.

Chapter 45

I MUST SAY BROATMARKLE is proving to be the ideal co-conspirator. He tacitly agrees that Stockhardt would distrust Julian boasting about sudden wealth on the first call, and that a cannier approach stands a much better chance of being believed. Toward that end, he arranged for Julian to phone his father outdoors, albeit inside the vehicle lockup adjacent to the detention center. The idea is for Julian to have fresh air, free hands, pacing room, and ambient noise.

This morning my stepbrother and I spent an hour alone in the interrogation room, covering and recovering the answers to whatever Stockhardt might conceivably ask. I hammered home that when he's on the phone, he is obviously *not* in lockup. Also, "Nobody has discovered the hair trophies in his backpack. Erased! You are a free man who has absolutely nothing to do with your mother's pretend murder. As far the world knows, you weren't even in Utah."

Sober, Julian was a pretty good study. Of course, freedom—even freedom with restrictions—is a powerful incentive. Negotiations with the state have been initiated by his overworked attorney, but the outcome largely depends on Julian's contribution to the case against Steven Stockhardt.

The upshot is that Julian, Broatmarkle, and I are enclosed in a parking lot with four black SUVs, three Hondas, one silver Cadillac, and two patrol cars. Surrounding us is a ten-foot high, razor topped, chain-link fence with a formidable gate.

With yesterday's clouds gone and no discernable breeze, we have hot blacktop underfoot. Leaning against a Honda, Broatmarkle regularly lifts his hat to wipe his face with his uniform sleeve. I'm twitching inside a light cotton top with a scratchy label, and Julian wears the expected jumpsuit and sliders on his feet with socks. His exposed skin shines with perspiration, but the main thing that's making all of us sweat is the critical phone call Julian's about to make.

The sergeant and I will listen in with earbuds attached to our phones via a connection some tech guy rigged. The call will also be recorded in the feeble hope that a forensics expert can pick up a clue as to Stockhardt's location.

I nod for Julian to go ahead, and he enters the direct number to his father on the burner phone in his hand. It's the one he had on him when he was arrested, the same one he used yesterday when Stockhardt hung up. Since he is dialing their exclusive number, the hope is that Stockhardt will answer again. However, it isn't inconceivable that the man doesn't plan to answer a call from Julian ever again. The first of many things that can go wrong today.

"Hello?"

One hurdle out of the way.

"Hey. It's me," Julian greets his father while rolling a loose stone under his jail-issued flip flop.

A natural enough beginning, but Stockhardt hesitates long enough for a generation of monks to build a cathedral.

When he finally asks, "How's your sister?" and Julian says, "She's a fucking bitch. You'd hate her guts," my shoulders dare to relax half an inch.

"I don't like this," Stockhardt says, huffing into his phone. "If the police were on yesterday's call, how can I be sure they're not on now?"

"They're not, okay? I'm on the loose. I'm in a fucking parking lot in the middle of a fucking city. Anyhow, you gave me this number. You tell me if it's safe."

A breathy sigh, then, "Yeah, okay. I just didn't expect to hear from you. What's with you and the police?"

"They think I know something about who killed Ma."

"And you thought it would be a good idea to call me."

Stockhardt's sarcasm landed on my chest like a load of rocks. I shake my hand to get Julian's attention, and the kid rolls his eyes.

"Here's the thing." He continues speaking confidentially, the way we rehearsed. "I found out Ma left me some money. A bank account I didn't even know was there, so I…"

"You what?"

I pat the air, reminding Julian not to say too much too fast.

"…so I just wanted to say we're good. No worries about the twenty. That's all."

Over by the Honda, Broatmarkle fans his face with his hat.

The kid forges ahead. "Yeah. Turns out Ma has…*had*….a savings account with my name on it. I can write checks and everything. Move the whole thing to another bank—whatever I want. I can't wait to trade in that shitty van…"

"How much?" Stockhardt interrupts.

"The new van…?"

"The bank account. How much are we talking about?"

The number Julian quotes is less than the grossly inflated, poolside lifestyle figure I made up to incentivize Stockhardt, which tells me Julian remains true to himself.

He's still the greedy little bastard he's been all along, and—despite what he just said—will never forgive his father for taking off without splitting that cash.

"Half!" Stockhardt echoes their original deal.

"Whaddya mean, half?"

"We split it half and half."

"Wow! I dunno. That's an awful lot…"

"Think of it this way. Share and we're both safe."

"Safe? I dunno, man."

"Julian," Stockhardt addresses his son the way real fathers are wont to do. "You're not seeing the big picture. With money like that I'm gone for good. Blow me off and the police get an anonymous tip about who killed your mother. Be smart, Julian. Take the deal."

Stockhardt's voice almost softens. "We've had a good run, Julian, you and me. But life is tough. You'll be okay. This is a no-brainer. Split the money and we'll both be better off."

"No."

NO? Julian actually said, "No." My heart is down at my feet.

Stockhardt mirrors my own reaction. "Don't be stupid, kid. You know I'm right."

Before I can begin to corral all the awful ramifications chasing around in my brain, Julian disconnects and tosses the phone to Broatmarkle.

Now he's walking toward the door to the lockup with his back toward me.

I've blocked his path and grabbed the front of the baggy jumpsuit before I realize what I've done.

"What's wrong with you?" I shout. "You screwed up everything!" His life. Any chance of putting Stockhardt behind bars. I'm so incensed my head is pounding.

"I didn't kill her," he yells right back. "Get outta my way."

That's it? He got caught up in his playacting, and for one horrifying moment believed it was okay to say no to Stockhardt—*because he didn't kill his mother*? Does he not understand that the probation Demming's trying to arrange depends entirely on him helping to bring about the arrest of a major criminal?

While our eyes still lock, all at once I see what happened.

Julian is right. He didn't kill his mother, so Stockhardt's threat to turn him in means nothing.

What set the kid off was something said without words. For Steven Stockhardt, ending their relationship would be as easy as stubbing out a cigarette.

I realize Broatmarkle is still here when he loosens my hands from Julian's jumpsuit. "Take it easy," he says. "We'll figure something out."

Julian's glare doesn't waver, and again he's got a point. There's no "we" about it.

This was all my idea, and it is a titanic failure.

Chapter 46

BROATMARKLE GUIDES HIS charge back into the building, leaving me to fend for myself.

I fumble my way back through the maze of security and sign myself out. My inclination is to head for the nearest burger joint for some high-calorie comfort. My head is swimming in recriminations, second and third guessing my apparently stupid plan. Why on earth did Broatmarkle listen to me? What made the guy agree to this terrible Hail-Mary move?

He thought it was a viable choice.

I'm standing on the steps where yesterday we watched the morning's watchers depart. Mirages waft off the vehicles in the parking lot. The leaves of the tall tree I consulted nap in desultory clumps.

I sit down on the top cement step.

I thought it was the only *viable choice, too.*

I am not really hungry, and I certainly don't want a drink. I want a solution to my screwup. Some way to make this right.

How, is the question.

People enter and exit the building, but I don't budge. One officer pauses to examine me with a professional eye, but, for the most part, they ignore the spacy woman with her chin on her fist.

The sun has dropped another increment toward the horizon before I realize what must be done.

I can scarcely wait to run it by Broatmarkle, but we are both visitors here, and asking for him inside would be a hassle.

Naturally, he seems to take forever to come out on his own. I picture him stopping for a chat, hitting the head, maybe buying a bottle of water from the vending machine.

"You're still here," he observes when he finally emerges. He doesn't ask why.

I stand and tug him away from the doorway. I don't want to be interrupted, and I'd rather not be overheard. Impatience makes me shift on my feet and clasp and unclasp my hands.

"Julian has to call Stockhardt again," I blurt.

Broatmarkle's hairy left eyebrow twitches. "Lauren, I know you tried. And I thought it was worth a shot, too, but…"

"…but don't you see? Julian's in the perfect position to call again. It would seem natural. Even more natural than the other calls. The kid's furious. He found out his father doesn't give a damn about him. What would you do if that happened to you?"

"Same as any other son," he answers almost without thought. "I'd bend over backwards to prove the son-of-a-bitch was wrong."

***

It's evening when Broatmarkle and I return to the lockup, and other than us the traffic is all employees. Stars spot the sky. A dusty breeze rattles the leaves on the tree out front. The sergeant and I have eaten a tasteless meal at the nearest diner. Julian…I don't know what he ate, but I hope it was crow.

The kid doesn't get to pace outside this time. He gets to sit in the unoccupied gym provided for the guards. It is empty but for us and smells like leather brined with sweat, an unmistakable odor that takes me back to when I was doing rehab.

My meeting with Julian is shorter and more forceful this time, with emphasis on the fact that he really, really screwed up this afternoon—and why. I can only pray that the message got through.

"You're going to have to be an Oscar-worthy actor tonight," I stress, elbows on my knees across facing wooden chairs brought in for the occasion.

"Be yourself, only totally convincing. I don't know how to put this except to tell you the truth. Your life depends on getting this right. You may not have killed your mother—big whoop—but you put your her in mortal danger and helped her rapist escape. You're lucky as hell Demming convinced a judge to forgive your part in that in exchange for Steven Stockhardt. The same Steven Stockhardt who put his hair trophies in your bag to frame *you* for at least five sexual assaults and probable murders. Let's not forget that. *Please* do not forget that."

"Alright, alright," Julian concurs. "Give it rest already. Steve is a total shit."

"Well, that's progress," I think aloud, as I lean back on my borrowed chair.

We go over the script another two times, until Broatmarkle becomes restless.

"You ready, kid?" he asks. "Because we can't be here all night."

Julian closes his eyes and holds out his hand for the cell phone.

Thus begins my second most terrifying twenty-minutes in recent memory, the first being rushing to the hospital to find out whether my father was still alive.

"Hey, it's me again," Julian tells his father unnecessarily when Stockhardt answers their private number.

"Yeah, so what?"

"Hey, don't be like that. I been thinkin,' and I think you're right. Like you said, I wasn't looking at the big picture. So, yeah. I get it. I'll split 50/50 like you said..."

"Whaddya know. You've got a brain between your ears."

I flap my hand for Julian's attention, widen my eyes.

"Here's the thing, Dad, er, uh, Steve...I'll float you the money—Mexico, Costa Rica, wherever you want to go..." Julian pauses to lick his lips.

"Good. That's good..." Stockhardt jumps in.

"...but, but...there's just one...Uh, here's the thing, uh Dad...I'm going with you."

Another cathedral gets built in France.

I circle my hand for Julian to continue.

"You there? You hear me? I'm going, too."

"Not a great idea," Stockhardt launches his objection. "I usually..."

"You're not listening, you're not *hearing* me. I'm coming with you. I'll pay, but wherever you're going, I'm going. You wanna disappear? Fine. I get it. But I need the cops off my back, too."

The next silence feels tremendous, like the massive low pressure before the skies open and just about drown you. And yet the conviction in Julian's voice is so implacable, were I Steven Stockhardt, I would brace myself for a deluge.

"Remember that last camping trip? Eh? Remember all the stuff you told me? Because I do. So, here's the thing. I know what you did, and you know what I did. Big f-ing deal. We stick together, nobody squeals on nobody. Right?"

"Are you threatening me, Julian? Because if you are..."

"No way, man. It's like you said. We stick together, we're both golden."

Waiting, I shut my eyes and support my head with my hands.

Then Stockhardt actually says what I never expected to hear.

"Okay, kid," he says. "Worth a try."

Chapter 47

"TUESDAY. MAYBE WEDNESDAY," was Stockhardt's evasive reply when Julian asked how soon they could meet, an answer that surprised nobody.

At our hasty meal just before the critical third phone call, Broatmarkle and I talked about a flexible, 24/7 location for Julian to wait for his father. I mentioned the hotel across from the restaurant where I first noticed Harold's gaudy circus trucks, and Broatmarkle liked its proximity to a Utah Highway Patrol barracks. For safety reasons, arresting a criminal inside a hotel isn't ideal, but the sergeant must have persuaded his superiors, because here we are.

For meeting up anytime day or night, Julian told Stockhardt there would be a room key waiting for him under an alias. Julian is still in lockup, of course, but I am here with a Utah Highway Patrolman at the ready next door. Broatmarkle checks in as often as possible. "Budget," the sergeant explained. "We have a whole state to protect, you know."

Yes, I know. And the drawbacks of greeting a killer mostly alone are enough to give me hives. Granted, the hotel security staff is watching their monitors for a tall, bearded man, or a tall man with a facial scar using the planned alias. But if Stockhardt slips by their notice, the state cop's warning—and mine—depend on the desk clerk alerting security that the key's been picked up, then security notifying us, a potentially worrisome delay.

In theory, I'm here by myself because a young, blonde woman alone in a hotel room is pretty much the opposite of threatening. How I field Stockhardt's entrance is up to me, but in my experience playing dumb, *really* dumb, is safest.

Other than that, we've staged the room as if a slob of a nineteen-year-old is sleeping and eating here. Clothes thrown on a chair, messy sink, towels on the bathroom floor, a duffle spewing dirty clothes in a corner. Depending on whether the maid is due, a rumpled bed.

Tuesday comes and goes like a wrench tightening a bolt. Our rotating Highway Patrol team members become increasingly uncertain about whether Stockhardt will show, also increasingly worried about his intentions.

By Wednesday afternoon, I catch myself yawning over a book as I lounge on the one soft chair the room provides. What the guy in the adjacent room is doing is impossible to guess. Playing solitaire? Napping? Learning how to make gnocchi on YouTube? All I hear is unnerving silence.

When late evening arrives, I keep my running shoes on for stability, but change into a slip-like nightie (hookers don't wear sweatpants) and a terrycloth bathrobe I bought downstairs. My loaded Glock fits inside the robe's cavernous pocket, but if I'm sitting it would be awkward to get out. Standing, the bulge might ruin my cover. Instead, I place it in the top drawer of the dresser to my immediate right, and keep the drawer slightly open.

As the hours stretch toward midnight, I leave the reading light on and place the book face down on my lap. I slept twice for an hour or two earlier in the day with the connecting door wide open and Broatmarkle on watch. But he's gone now, and night is seductive. It's tough not to doze.

The beep of the keycard going green and the click of the door softly brushing across the carpet frighten me to attention.

"Julie?" I call out sleepily. "Did you get some?" Drugs, condoms, beer—whatever blank Stockhardt's brain fills in doesn't matter, but forewarning him that I'm not Julian does.

I wonder. Does my state-cop babysitter next door know that a killer is inching toward me *RIGHT NOW*?

"Who are you?" Stockardt asks with an insistence bordering on malice.

He is indeed tall, with a mop of dirty blonde hair, and a beard that appears more unshaven than planned. He carries no luggage or bag of any sort, which—along with arriving in the dead of night—telegraphs that he is not here to give Julian a fatherly hug. "We've had a good run, Julian, you and me. But life is tough," Stockhardt told his biological son even before Julian's, "You know what I did, and I know what you did," threat.

"Did the kid invite you," I ask back, "because that'll cost more."

Stockhardt's right hand is hidden behind his back. His empty left dangles alongside his pocket, where he probably deposited the key card. Fingerprints. DNA. Criminals are well-aware.

Dominant hand? No way to tell.

I am standing now, as any woman would be confronting a stranger in the middle of the night. Sneakered feet apart. Fists at my sides.

Stockhardt's right hand stays put as he saunters closer, so I'm thinking, "knife," the quietest way to kill with people sleeping nearby.

"Where's Julian?"

"Condoms," I respond with a tense laugh. "We ran out."

"Ummm," Stockhardt pretends to muse, then surprises me with a backhand across my jaw.

I grab the arm as it passes, but the blow lands hard.

While the headrush floods my brain, a knife flashes before my eyes.

"Who are you?" Stockhardt repeats.

I spit blood on the floor. Summon up some attitude. "I'm the Easter bunny."

The knife tip rises to touch my chin. "My son would never, ever, touch a whore. Try again."

Dang. I was so used to working Vice, I forgot Daddy's campsite lectures about tainted women.

"I'm Lauren. Lauren, the bitch." And where the hell is my backup? Stockhardt might quit talking and slit my throat any second now.

He huffs out a nasty smile.

"Where's Julian?"

"He's a little afraid of you," I waffle, which should be true, but may not be the right thing to say. "But no worries. He'll be right back…" I quickly add.

Suddenly the connecting door slams open. The state cop jumps in, shouts "Freeze," and points his gun our way.

Stockhardt's eyes shift off my face ever so briefly, but long enough for me to move. Pivoting to my right, I punch the back of his right wrist while stomping on his foot with most of my weight. The mechanics of the punch loosen his grasp, and the knife falls to the carpet. The stomp pains him enough to throw him off balance.

The Utah cop tries another shout, but with me in his firing range, the warning has no effect.

Stockhardt sees that I'm reaching toward the dresser, glimpses the gun, and gets there first.

I kick the drawer shut on his hand, but fall backward onto the chair.

My backup is still in his two-handed, gun-pointing, "You're under arrest," stance, but Stockhardt doesn't care. He got the Glock after all, and is aiming right back.

Standoff?

Not quite. I grab the reading lamp and hit Stockardt's back with the base.

A shot is fired as he goes down.

The broken lamp puts us in the dark, and I can't tell what condition the perp is in. He's twitching as I fumble for the side of his neck, find his carotid, press as hard as I can, and wait for the bastard to pass out.

From the sound of heavy feet running out in the hall, somebody is on the way.

The night security man lets himself in. Flips on the overhead and gasps.

"An ambulance would be good," I remark to his open mouth. Blood is pouring onto the carpet from Stockhardt's thigh.

"Yeah. Yeah. I'm on it."

Meanwhile, the Utah cop, whose name turns out to be Ted, gets a tourniquet from his kit and uses it on Stockhardt. The crisp snap of handcuffs is music to my ears.

"By the way," I address the house detective after I've stood and tightened the bathrobe. "Where was my signal?"

Ted retrieves my phone from the spot on the floor where it fell, taps the screen, and shows me there is none. The receptionist who should have alerted security—didn't.

I ask how he knew Stockhardt was here.

"Had the TV on mute. Heard voices."

Even money he was watching sports, which seem to be perpetually on. "Your team win?"

He glances toward the bleeding man lying on the floor. "I'd say so, wouldn't you?"

Chapter 48

I'VE BEEN BACK at Dad and Ana's for four days now. Fall is settling in. Coupons for Halloween candy galore. A hint of cooler air. The hope of a little rain in the forecasts.

The news about Steven Stockhardt's arrest has finally disappeared from the headlines, but that doesn't mean more revelations won't be forthcoming. The girl who escaped her potential rapist will have an opportunity to pick him out of a photo array. In support of Julian's claim that his father planted damning evidence in his backpack, Stockhardt's DNA can now be compared to that on the twist tie holding the hair trophies together.

Already, Sergeant Broatmarkle let me know that none of Stockhardt's trophies link my "billboard girl" Kathleen Duncan to Stockhardt. Cheryl Anderson's daughter remains a possibility yet to be proven.

Heartbreaking news. Kelly Sethi's wavy black hair is a bonafide match. She's the nine-year-old who disappeared while walking a dog outside a Salt Lake City mall. The authorities checked, and Julian has a solid alibi for that time and place—further confirmation that the trophies found in his backpack were not his.

The Sethi match also pares down the hunt for Stockhardt's other victims to the Amber-alert age range, and narrows the geographic area to abductions occurring in Utah and the adjoining southwestern states—at least temporarily. Considering that Stockhardt raped Ana twenty years ago, it's likely other trophies exist, something the authorities have in mind.

Ana checked in with Demming yesterday. Yes, she kept the beleaguered, court-appointed attorney, and why not? He's arranging probation—exactly what she and Julian want. Apparently, negotiations are especially slow-going because both Utah and New Mexico need to agree, the latter because Julian will be residing with his mother and my dad. Probationers must also get a job, which makes the arrangement sound somewhat long term.

I will be leaving before he arrives, because (a) the house isn't big enough for two guests, and (b) I would rather jump off a cliff than be in Julian Tomas's presence again.

In all fairness, I got him and his father arrested, so he probably feels the same.

Then there's Ana and me. In order to apprehend the man who corrupted Julian, framed him for his many crimes, and was prepared to kill her, I got Ana to remember her rape—in detail, which will probably require some serious therapy. Most likely, my new stepmother isn't completely pleased by that outcome. Throw in that my presence is a daily reminder of her latest traumatic experience, and it's understandable that our relationship is a bit…uncomfortable.

With nothing to lose, I might as well take a stab at détente while I'm still here.

Dad and I have just finished a late breakfast, but Ana has probably been closeted away in her studio for a couple of hours. To her, meals seem to have become optional.

Placing a croissant on a paper plate, I tap on her door.

No answer, so I open it a crack and poke my head in.

The large room is loaded with pieces in progress, shelves and tables full of equipment and tools. In one corner a kiln, another a wheel, toward the center something flat, perhaps for rolling clay. The belongings I tucked against the wall when I first arrived are now covered with a fine, white dust.

"Mind if I see what you're making?"

Ana's head jerks up as if I pulled her mind out of a riveting thriller. She answers with a tepid, "Okay."

I set the paper plate on the cleanest spot I can find.

"One of your abstracts?" I query, regarding the clay in her hand. Dad told me more than a hundred pieces go into her elaborate designs.

"Um humm," she says, holding something up to the light.

Strolling around like a prospective customer, a scrapbook on a shelf catches my eye.

"May I?"

"Sure."

Inside are photos of past projects, the colorful, decidedly Southwestern/Mexican masterpieces for which Ana is becoming known. Flipping through page after page of jaw-droppingly beautiful designs, I blurt, "No wonder you're so famous!"

Only yesterday she was commissioned to produce a "significant" piece to commemorate a Mexican museum's upcoming centennial. Astonished and overjoyed, she and Dad clasped arms and bounced up and down laughing. I felt invisible. As if were already back east.

"Oh no, not really," she demurs now, modestly fluttering a hand toward the door.

So much to say to each other, and no idea how to start.

To hide my discomfort, I rummage through my duffel and extract a nicer shirt than the one I'm wearing. Then I wipe my feet on the mat by the door and excuse myself.

Ana doesn't seem to hear.

I change shirts and return to the kitchen. Pour myself half a cup of cold coffee. Drink it in long gulps.

Peering at me over the newspaper, Dad remarks, "You look nice. You goin' somewhere?"

"Out!" I respond like the teenager I once was.

Dad shakes out the sports page. "Where to?" he inquires, like the father he still is.

"I have an appointment."

"Oh, an *appointment*," he teases. "Getting your hair done?"

"Like I ever…"

"Meeting a guy?"

He's close, so I just say, "Yup," and dig out my car keys.

Chapter 49

WITHOUT SO MUCH as a handshake, Jack Jenkins greets me outside the designated convenience store a mile away from the used-car lot. He fans his face with his hat as he vouches for me to the two New Mexico state cops he seems to know personally.

"You comin' along, Jack?" asks the freckled one.

"Just for fun?" jokes the one with white hair.

"Sure. Strictly an observer, of course. This is your bailiwick."

"Bailiwick?" I ask with my face.

Jack just smiles and replaces his hat. "We should hit the road. These guys are expensive."

"You ain't exactly starving, Chief." Whitey chuckles as he turns toward their squad car.

The dust remains thick on the car-dealer's inventory, and the multicolored flags above barely wiggle in the still air. My beloved Miata is absent. We've both moved on.

Even without my striped tank top and shorts, the salesman I nicknamed Ernie recognizes me. Resplendent in today's pea-green sport coat, he races across the gleaming floor to greet me as if he harbors no hard feelings—toward anybody ever.

"How's the Jeep?" he inquires, fingering his tie as he speaks. "No problems, I hope."

"Just one. It's complicated. I think I should talk to your mechanic myself, if you don't mind."

Concerned that I might become difficult again, Ernie hedges. "He's in the middle of something. Why don't you tell Glenda over there all about it, and she'll take a look at the schedule."

"I want to speak to the mechanic. Now."

"How about the manager?" Ernie suggests.

I used my most assertive voice. Maybe it was too much.

"The mechanic, please. It'll only take ten minutes." Maybe less. But then they'll need a new mechanic.

"Is this about the…?" Ernie seems to have caught a bit of motion outside the showroom's glass wall. I don't turn to look, but it has to be Jack or one of his state highway patrol buddies.

The jingle bell on the entrance door alerts the salesmen, me, and probably the manager, too.

"The mechanic, please," I repeat.

"Right," Ernie answers, but he's gawping at something beyond my shoulder.

Hearing leather footsteps, I look over to see Jack wandering toward a bank of waiting-room seats. He settles down as if he's early for picking up his car. Rolls his hat between his hands. Looks innocent as a crocodile.

Ernie takes longer than expected, but he does return with the mechanic, hustling alongside the bigger man and yakking all the way.

The mechanic's body language says he would like to swat Ernie.

I'd been standing sideways to them, but now I square myself across their path.

Ernie pivots on a toe and makes straight for his desk.

The mechanic halts so fast his head snaps forward. Filthy tan XL overalls hang loosely across his sloped shoulders. The thin fingertips of the right hand by his side are spatulate and darkened with grease. The other hand is bandaged. Beneath messy dark hair are the earlobes I remember, oddly squared off as if by scissors.

Today, I recognize the signs of plastic surgery I missed before, tight cheeks and an absence of wrinkles around the eyes. Inappropriate for the age I know the man to be. Appropriate for someone in the Witness Protection program.

We stand a mere twelve feet apart, closer than gunslingers at high noon. If he wants to lunge for my throat, he'll make it, but only if I stand still.

"Hello, JB," I greet him.

His chin jerks upward.

His free hand flexes. His chest heaves. His eyes are so filled with hate he looks like a furnace about to explode.

Behind him, the two New Mexico cops have entered via the drop-off tunnel and are easing to the left and back of the mechanic. Jack Jenkins is gravitating toward us.

"JB for Jailbait," I repeat. "Isn't that what your bosses nicknamed you before you ratted them out?" By reputation, the man was a remarkably inept criminal. To his mob superiors, the "underage girl" implication was an extra laugh—an additional insult for the man to resent.

"What do you want?" he demands, each word clipped, insistent, and menacing.

"Your cell phone," I reply, hoping to throw my former arrestee off for a second.

He glances side to side. Something's about to give, but it isn't what I expect.

"Give it to her."

I've been so fixated on the mechanic I didn't notice Rollie Holcroft's silent approach. So far, the Jeep's former owner remains unaware of his employee's criminal history—ideally how Witness Protection is supposed to work.

JB, real name Gregorio Malford, glares at his current boss with disbelief.

The state cops don't wait. Swiftly moving in, they grab the mechanic's arms and twist them behind his back.

Fighting restraint, JB swears that, "I should have killed you on sight."

Paunched and florid as ever, Rollie remains unfazed. He strolls right up to his employee, pats the bucking suspect's overall pockets, and extracts a cell phone.

Holding it aloft as if two brawny state cops weren't wrestling a six-foot-tall bear just past his elbow, Holcroft offers it to me. "This what you want?"

"Yes, thanks." I tap it on with a trembling fingertip, hold it to its owner's face for recognition, then swipe across the icons until I find the tracking app. The state's tech team should be able to retrieve the device's history. Within a few feet, it will reveal everywhere the Jeep has been since the day I bought it. Most important, it will pinpoint where my father stopped to buy lunch the day he was shot.

I nod to the two cops that we have what we need, and Whitey starts reciting the message. "Gregorio Malford, you are under arrest for the attempted murder of Bernard Beck..." not to mention multiple attacks on me. "You have the right to..."

Gregorio does not remain silent. He struggles mightily to free his arms, all the while shouting about how some "blankety-blank bitch of a cop" ruined his life.

"Stop that," Whitey demands with a raised taser.

Malford recognizes defeat when he sees it.

The cops move to hustle him away, but I raise my hands to stall them.

He's not going to like a word I say, but I feel it's only fair to tell him the truth.

"Your partner..."

"Charles," Malford snaps. "Use his name."

"Yes. Charles asked me to tell you he was staying in Philadelphia because he knew you'd try to change his mind. He had ALS, Greg, and he wanted to stay near his friends and family. He was afraid if he told you himself, you'd refuse to go into Witness Protection, and your life would have been in constant danger."

Beyond frustrated and angry, the man literally erupts. Claiming over and over that I should have told him, he growls and spits and swears and vigorously fights his restraints until the officers literally have to drag him out the door. Were he loose to kill me, I feel certain he would have succeeded.

"You okay?" It's Jack being solicitous.

I say I'm fine, "just glad it's against the law to kill a messenger."

Chapter 50

JACK AND I are outside the used car dealership breathing dust and the smell of plastic, possibly from the fading flags overhead.

"Sorry," he begins. "I'm afraid the state cops want your Jeep for a few days. Forensics needs to examine the tracking device in situ."

"In situ?" I tease.

"Larry reads books."

"Good for him."

"So, hop in," he suggests, gesturing toward his squad car. "I'm your ride home."

Relaxing in the passenger seat, I roll my head trying to unwind. Wiggle my shoulders.

As we pull onto the highway heading back toward Albuquerque, I lament how slow I was catching onto Gregorio.

"You were busy," Jack reminds me. "How did you finally figure it was him?"

"The phony drug store story first, I guess. I always thought he made that up just to keep his job."

"Agreed."

"But then…," I drew out the drama, "…*then* I wondered why the Jeep? He was surrounded by cars. If his mission was that urgent, why not borrow one of them?"

"…because the mission had something to do with you."

"Yep. He'd just been face to face with the bitch who wrecked his life, and he couldn't let me get away. Putting a tracker on the Jeep was the answer, but he didn't have one handy. Maybe he already had one on his truck, but he'd lent that to somebody for the day. Or maybe he knew where to buy one quick. Doesn't matter. You know the rest."

As we ride through the desolate landscape in silence, my hyped-up mind is performing somersaults.

When I can contain myself no longer, I tell Jack I have an idea.

"Not again."

We smile at each other. Platonically, of course.

"I'm tired of criminals," I say. "You must be, too. How about we do something for a victim instead?"

I explain how I felt compelled to visit Cheryl Anderson, the stranger whose daughter was abducted from a campground near Yellowstone National Park. She felt alone, I was told. Her friends tried, but weren't really much help. The detective who gave me her name thought Cheryl might appreciate the company of someone who shared her pain. "As it turned out, we both got something out of the visit.

"Doesn't Kathleen Duncan's family live somewhere between here and Albuquerque?"

"Yes, Polly and Dan. Dan does not like cops."

"Will he be home?"

"Probably not, but I'd rather not raise Polly's hopes."

"So, tell her up front you don't have any new information. Just say you'd like stop by and see how she's doing. Please? I've been wanting to do this ever since I saw that billboard, and it's right on our way."

"You need an introduction."

"If you want to put it that way, yes."

Jack grumbles, but he humors me and makes the call. I'm not sure why Kathleen's mother agrees to our visit, but she does.

We arrive at the Duncan's parched bungalow about four p.m. A constant breeze blows hot and dusty across the nearby desert, drying our nostrils and eyes and urging us inside as soon as possible.

Polly, a generously endowed woman in a tight pink t-shirt and cutoff jeans opens the door with weary distrust, and I instantly suspect depression. It's in the dullness of her eyes, the creases of her cheeks, the hang of her arms. Even in the slow way she moves aside to let us enter her home.

"Hello, Polly," Jack greets her, taking her hand and holding it affectionately for a moment.

The woman's eyes lift with a tiny spark of pleasure and surprise, solving the mystery of why she agreed to see us on short notice. Any sort of attention from Jack Jenkins is welcome here.

"This is a friend of mine, Lauren Beck. She's former police from Pennsylvania. She wanted to meet you and pay her respects."

Polly's gaze leaves Jack long enough to spare me a puzzled squint.

"Thank you for letting me come, Ms. Duncan," I tell her. "I saw your daughter's billboard when I arrived here, and I've been thinking of Kathleen ever since."

"Okay."

We've gravitated the few feet across the living room, stopping at a rustic pine coffee table littered with movie magazines, a bowl of cigarette butts, and a leftover beer can.

She gestures us into two mismatched wooden side chairs. Between them rests a print sofa so old and worn that after our host plops herself onto its cushions, smoke and dust join the sour body odor and other smells permeating the room. Likely culprits? The dishes piled in the sink and on the kitchen counter spanning the cottage's short back wall. The single window above is likely opaque with cigarette and cooking residue.

Hat between his hands, Jack leans forward to rest his elbows on his knees.

"How are you doing, Polly?"

The woman flashes him an electric look that instantly defaults to dejection.

Jack appears to address his hat. "I'm sorry we couldn't do more," he admits. "It's a failure that haunts everyone in my department." He glances toward me. "Lauren experienced a similar loss."

"You lost a daughter?"

"No, Ms. Duncan," I reply. "I had a bad experience when I was police, that's all. It haunts me, though, and I keep wanting to do something…whatever I can to comfort anyone going through what you are."

"And you think that helps?"

"That's not for me to say. I just want you to know that whenever a case is unresolved, especially ones involving children, we can't forget, and we don't. I know for certain Jack will never stop trying to find your daughter."

"What's left to do?" the grieving mother asks, directing the question to him.

Quick, before he begins his mollifying answer, I ask Polly if it would be okay if I used their bathroom. "It's been a long drive…"

"Sure. Sure, go ahead."

I rise just as the front door slams open, and a drunk man storms in.

"What's with the cop car? Huh, Polly? D'you call 'em?"

Dan Duncan is a big lug, as sloppy as his wife, and belligerent as a bull. His plaid shirt flaps over a dingy t-shirt. Below—work boots and jeans. His facial skin glistens over a dark, two-day shadow. On our way here, Jack related that Dan is a handyman for a real estate conglomerate, which means odd hours and uncertain pay. The job also offers the flexibility to ignore his homelife and yield to his chosen escape—gambling on pool hall games played against other malcontents as angry and thwarted as he.

"Just checking in to see how y'all are doing, Dan," Jack addresses Kathleen's father. "Join us here," he suggests, indicating the sofa. "Tell me how you two are faring."

I stopped in my tacks when the door opened, but the police chief lifts his chin to shoo me along, quick before we get kicked out on our asses.

"Fuck that," Dan Duncan retorts to Jack's opening as he bee-lines to the clunking refrigerator for a beer.

"You been playin' pool again?" Polly accuses from her spot on the couch.

"What's it to you? You been sittin' on your ass as usual?"

I don't hear much more, because I've slipped into Kathleen's bedroom and partially closed the door behind me.

The room is teenage-girlie on a shoestring. Pink walls, a bottle of pink nail polish on a desk fifteen inches deep, no wider than a yard. Pinned to the cork board above are photos of Kathleen and a girlfriend hamming it up in a photo booth, Kathleen with two others in bathing suits posing like movie stars alongside a crowded swimming pool. A calendar of kitten pictures remains pinned open to August of the previous year. The closet is supplied with just enough clothes suitable for school—a couple sweaters, an extra pair of jeans, and a skirt and blouse for dressing up. The jewelry box on Kathleen's white, four-drawer dresser contains bracelets made of tiny pink beads and a string of fake pearls, such as a young teen might wear to church. A cardboard strip poked with holes holds a handful of earrings. The only lampshade is white, as is the filmy curtain scantly covering a yellowed window shade.

I emerge not much wiser than I entered, knowing only that Kathleen Duncan was an ordinary fourteen-year-old girl when she disappeared over a year ago…and that she is still missing.

When I return to the living room, Dan is sitting with one arm draped across his wife's soft shoulders, his free hand surrounding an open beer.

Polly's raised eyebrow suggests she saw me emerge from Kathleen's room.

"I hope you don't mind that I took a quick peek," I say with a weak smile. "Her room is so…so feminine."

"Yeah, like mother, like daughter," drunken Dan remarks, plucking at his wife's pink t-shirt like a mischievous adolescent. Then he looks me right in the eye as if he's made a monumental observation.

Which he has.

"Jack!" I urge, but the police chief is in quiet conversation with Polly again.

"Jack! We gotta go. Thanks for letting us visit, Polly, Dan," I effuse. "You've been very…hospitable. Jack!"

He finally catches on.

Thank yous and goodbyes completed, he stops me just outside the Duncan's disheveled marriage on the doorstep of their disheveled house.

"What?" he demands.

"In the car," I stall. "Let's get moving."

"What?" he insists as soon as the car doors clunk shut.

He's right. He shouldn't be driving while he listens to this.

As I finish, his mouth draws into the classic O of awe. He spends another few seconds staring at the horizon, then reaches down to start the car.

Dad and Ana's home is miles away, but he drives the entire distance without uttering a single word.

"Good luck!" I call after his exiting vehicle, for I gave Jack Jenkins a lot to do.

An enormous amount, as it happens.

Chapter 51

DEMMING FINALLY COMPLETED the paperwork on Julian's probation yesterday at noon, and by two Ana had an overnight bag packed. She left for Utah to bring her son home soon after sunrise today.

This morning I washed my sheets and remade my borrowed bed. I wiped down the bathroom to erase any hint that I so much as crossed its threshold. I cleaned up the kitchen after Dad and I had one final lunch, and we just finished loading the Jeep.

My throat aches with the thought of parting with my father. I'll always tell him where I am and what I'm up to, and trust he'll do the same. Yet I'm afraid the complexity of my relationship with Ana may interfere. He's with her now, as he should be. As he wants to be.

It's up to me to create my own life. Too bad I don't have a clue what that will look like, no clue even what I want beyond tomorrow.

The other day when Jack—that sweet, beautiful, happily married man—offered me a job, we both burst out laughing.

"Friends," I suggested instead, and he agreed.

"Does this mean I can call you anytime day or night?"

"Absolutely not," he replied. "Seriously, Lauren. If there's anything I can do for you, just call the station."

"During working hours."

"Yes, please."

We shook on that.

***

My dad is only using one crutch today, giving that a whirl. He stands just outside the bright blue front door where I was mugged the night I arrived, smiling at me wistfully.

I'm about to tease him about the wrinkle cream, deliver the line I've rehearsed for my perfect-for-us departure.

My mouth opens, but when I glance up, I see pain on his face that has nothing to do with his leg. Nothing to do with Ana either. It has something to do with me.

"I haven't been honest with you, Beanie," he says, confirming my fear, "and I'm so, so sorry."

I draw back. "What do you mean? I think we've always been pretty straight with each other. Maybe a little white lie now and then, but never over anything important…"

Dad is waiting for me to stop.

When I finally do, he lifts his damp eyes and instantly puts tears in mine.

"Your mother isn't dead, Beanie," he says, waving his head. "At least I don't think so. We've been out of touch for years…"

"What do you mean, not dead? How can that be?"

Dad's face is flushed now, his expression tortured. Whatever he's about to tell me, it appears he's to blame.

"I… I…"

"What did you do?" I demand.

He pauses a moment to squint his eyes. "I threw her out."

"But…why?" I'm reeling now, almost in need of a crutch myself.

"She hit you, Beanie. She was drunk, and she hit you. I couldn't let that happen again, so I threw her out."

I stagger back a step, drop my purse to the ground.

"I'm sorry I didn't tell you before, but the time never seemed right. Your mother's an alcoholic, Lauren, an unhappy, out of control, alcoholic. She tried rehab twice that I know of, but the first one didn't stick. I don't know about the second. The last I saw her was after our divorce became final and she picked up some of her stuff. I let you kids think she died so you wouldn't waste any time hoping for her to come back."

"I don't remember her hitting me. Why don't I remember that?"

But maybe now I did. A blow across my ear that knocked me flat. Band-Aids on my hands and cheek.

"So, all those questions I was asking. Why didn't you tell me then?"

He waves his head again. "It was the last one that got me."

The last...?

Dad answers before I can remember.

"You're nothing like her, Beanie. Not one bit."

Chapter 52

WHEN MY CELL PHONE shows who's calling, I'm on Route 40, aka Route 66, headed west, still undecided about whether to aim for the Painted Desert, the Grand Canyon, or Coconino National Forest. It's almost dinnertime, and I've been keeping an eye out for a burger joint with milkshakes. So far, all I've seen is lots of bleak, rugged countryside.

Knowing what I'm about to hear, I take the first opportunity to pull off the highway, onto the parched, empty exit ramp for Grants, New Mexico. I've scarcely eased off the tarmac and brought "Buck" a stop when another car whizzes past, rocking the Jeep and blowing dust into my open window.

Which I quickly close. I also shut off the engine for what will surely be a difficult talk.

"Hi, Dad."

"Julian's been arrested for murder," my father blurts without preamble. "You know anything about that?" He sounds shocked, maybe a little angry, too. Hard to tell.

"Yes, Dad, I know. The girl's name is Kathleen Duncan."

Among other things, I told Jack Jenkins that Julian's probation requires him to live with his mother and my dad for the foreseeable future, which allowed the local authorities to wait for Julian to return to their jurisdiction. It also permitted the specialists to lock down their evidence—like yesterday.

"You had something to do with this?" Dad demands. "Why didn't you warn me?"

"And how would that have worked out? Hmmm?" He would have told Ana…Ana would have warned Julian…

A heavy sigh suggests Dad connected those dots and moved on.

"Ana's fit to be tied, Beanie," he bemoans, revealing his major concern. "I honestly don't know what to do with her."

"You're her husband. You'll figure it out."

"I'm gonna have to. Thanks to you."

"He's guilty, Dad."

"And you know this how?"

"You probably didn't see it yet, but Julian wears a pink stud earring. Its exact mate was found under Kathleen's remains."

During our first interview with Julian at the detention center, he remarked that his father had a predilection for young girls, but it's unlikely that was the end of their conversation. How tempting it must have been for Stockhardt to brag about his secret conquests to someone who would never tell—his protégé, the son he had already groomed into a rapt admirer. Even at the age thirteen or fourteen, Julian would easily have figured out why his hero's victims would never talk.

"Is that all they've got?" Dad asks regarding the evidence against Ana's son.

"No. It'll all come out during the trial."

This time my father's sigh is from exasperation. "You'll be here to testify?"

"No."

"Then what exactly is your part in this?"

"You won't tell Ana?"

"God, no."

"I had an epiphany."

"What the hell does that mean?"

He doesn't need a dictionary; he's demanding every last detail.

To pacify him, I describe the whole visit with the Duncans, ending with Dan's, "Like mother, like daughter…"

"And…?"

"And it made me think of you and Ron."

"For heaven's sake, Lauren. What can we possibly have to do with a dead girl from Albuquerque, New Mexico?"

A truck speeds by, pelting the Jeep's door with dirt.

"Nothing," I answer. "It just made me wonder. Of all the occupations in the world, why did Ron go into farming?"

"He knows farming. He loves farming."

"Correct. But you were a farmer. In a way, isn't it possible he's also honoring you? And if that's possible, couldn't there also be a flipside?"

I tell Dad that after Jack Jenkins and I finished at the used car dealer's, we visited the home of Kathleen Duncan, "the girl on the billboard near where my car broke down." I explain how I got to see the missing girl's bedroom, and that it was almost entirely pink.

"When the father plucked at his wife's pink t-shirt and said, 'Like mother, like daughter,' I thought of the first time I met Julian. His pink earring stood out as such an odd choice that, even then, I thought it might have some special significance.

"That extra-long camping trip bothered me, too. Six weeks of 24/7 exposure to Stockhardt's sociopathic views on women, domination, and sex? What if Julian came away from that with more than just a warped education? What if he also came away with intent?"

Sitting in the patrol car outside the Duncans' house, I shared all my presumptions with Jack.

And just as I hoped and expected, he and his department did a spectacular job of following through. Officers revisited Kathleen's school friends with new, more specific, questions and a photo array of possible suspects. One girl identified Julian as someone she saw hanging around outside their school.

Julian's local friends were also tracked down and quizzed about his activities around the time of the abduction. A swarthy, unkempt fellow not unlike Ana's son related that he and Julian sometimes "partied" in the desert at night. Stoned out of their minds, they lay on top of the white van staring at the stars for hours.

"Recently?"

"Nah. Not for a year or so."

Shown a map, the party-friend made his best guess as to where they'd been. The area wasn't small, but it was limited enough for Jack to get approval for a drone search. Within two days, the search revealed the nearly mummified remains of Kathleen Duncan.

Jack kept me apprised of his team's progress, mostly by text, now and then with a call when something especially promising turned up. The inclusion was a subtle form of thanks, which is more than enough recognition for me. Let Jack Jenkins dominate the news cycle like a handsome cross between Einstein and Houdini. I'm on my way to Yellowstone.

Yes, definitely Yellowstone.

"Julian claims it was an accident," my father remarks.

"They all say that, Dad. Was it an accident to leave her body in the desert?"

"Seriously, Beanie, that's how you think? Sometimes I don't know you at all."

"You know I'm not like my mother."

"Am I going to be sorry I told you that?"

"Nope. I'm good. How about you?"

"All in, Beanie. Keep in touch, will you? It can be tough out there."

"Will do. Hey! I've got a question."

"Shoot."

"How does wrinkle cream know how to fill the cracks but leave the rest of your face alone?"

"Goodbye, Beanie."

"Bye, Dad. Love you."

"Ditto."

#

Pretty please!

If you enjoyed STRANGER DANGER, a quick and easy way to pay it forward is to leave a **brief review** on its product page wherever you buy books online. Prospective readers will welcome another mystery fan's opinion, and I'll appreciate the feedback, too. Double win!

Interested in being the first to hear about a special bargain, a new release, a tempting contest, or maybe just some good news?

Please join my **Mystery Guest list** (gift involved). Link on my website: **donnahustonmurray.com.**

Many thanks!

Donna

Acknowledgements

Many thanks to this bunch of wonderful people who generously contributed to STRANGER DANGER, each in their own special way: Robynne Graffam, my superb editor; Dione Benson, a proofreader I heartily recommend; Michelle Argyle, my indispensable cover artist, and these patient and kind Beta readers—Hench Murray, Elissa Strati, George Reese, Paul Schlecker, Bernadette Cinkoske, Kate Mahalik, and Katie Miller Norrell.

Others who shared their special expertise: Dr. Ken Zamkoff; Dr. Jodi Mullen, and Jennifer Angelier, both of whom I met on airplanes (it pays to chat up your seatmates!); Jackie Spiller, Maria Pappas, and LuAnne Lunger of Santander Bank; plus potters extraordinaire Phil Henderson and Ralph Levy. I also used the Peter's Place website, and got excellent advice from Joy Haynie and Joseph Minissale.

I especially enjoyed interviewing Oscar P. Vance, Jr., M.S. C.H.T.. Speaking with him was an inspiration and a delight, and I hope he forgives me for how I used his information.

Donna Huston Murray's cozy mystery series features an amateur sleuth much like herself, a DIY headmaster's wife with a troubling interest in crime. The latest Gin Barnes' FOR BETTER OR WORSE was a Finalist for the *National Indie Excellence Award* for mysteries, and both novels in her new mystery/crime series won Honorable Mention in genre fiction from *Writer's Digest.*

In 2022, Donna became the tenth inductee into her high school's **Lifetime Achievement Award Hall of Fame**. To hint that she's still writing, the plaque reads, "…and more," below her listed books.

When she isn't plotting mayhem, Donna assumes she can fix anything until proven wrong, calls trash-picking recycling, and, although she should probably know better by now, adores Irish setters.

Donna and husband, Hench, live in the greater Philadelphia, PA, USA, area.

Made in the USA
Middletown, DE
30 March 2023

27917799R00149